Fishbowl

International, Inc.

Grandmama's
Mojo
STILL Working

Sydney Molare'

ISBN: 0-9745188-8-3

LCCN: 2004112441

First Printing: October 2004

Fishbowl International, Inc.
PO Box 362
Roxie, MS 39661
www.fishbowlinternational.com

Other works by Sydney Molare'

Somewhere In America

Changing Faces, Changing Places

Small Packages

This book is dedicated to Lindsey, LaKendria, Ariel, Janna, Katlyn, Jada, LaJoi, and Sydney

Sweeties, please **Read** this book as many times as necessary; **Remember** the lessons and wisdom within; and **Respect** yourself enough to demand respect from those around you.

I love you guys always,

Mama and "T"

Grandmama's
Mojo
STILL Working

www.sydneymolare.com

Fishbowl International, Inc.

Ode to Madame A

Listen my sisters and hear what I say
Of the words of wisdom from Madame A
Brown as a bean, hips wide as the sea
Words exit her lips stopping the air around thee
Short of stature she stands, but this does deceive
Ask men snared by her mojo, powerless to leave
Bottle up her essence, sell it on the street
Be the first to get the patent, millionaire within a week
No roots, potions or Ms. Cleo by her side
From years of experience does her knowledge lie
Back unbowed by mind slavery induced by a man
Unenslavement of the mind she preaches wherever she
can
Words to inspire, promote, but never demean
Kick him to the curb if he can't treat you like The Queen
Oh the tears that flow from our crying eyes
When we give our all in spite of his obvious lies
One won't act right, another one will
Either way, you'll be breathing still
Flip the script, jump backwards, turn it around
Then you'll be on the road, freedom bound
Disbelieve me if you want, but please hear what I say
"Heed the wise words from Madame A!"

Sydney M.

Grandmama's Mojo

CHAPTER

1

Exotic?

I stare again at the photo in the book I'd been reading. The caption beneath the picture described this 'perfect' model as six-foot one, one hundred ten pounds and "exotic" looking. Staring at facial features strongly resembling an armadillo, I'm convinced that "exotic" is a nice way of saying ugly, because this chick is past ugly. She is you-gly! And how many grown women still weigh one hundred ten pounds and don't have a terminal illness? What's wrong with being thick like me?

Disgusted, I toss the book, *The Lane to Personal Perfection,* across the room; barely missing the trashcan I was aiming for. Who writes all these stupid things anyway? My face scrunches up as I suddenly remembered *why* I was reading the book in the first place. Stefan, my friend—he insists that boyfriend is such an outdated term so we stick to friend—suggested it, along with the others I had been reading for the past two months. He said that the women in these books were the kind he was looking to share the rest of his life with. Well I definitely want to be the one he picks. Unfortunately, none of them were even remotely like me.

I'm only a freshman here at Magnolia A & M but Stefan is a *junior*. A fine, sexy junior with curly black hair, light brown eyes, and a bomb of a ride—a 2003 maroon Camaro. We've been seeing each other off and on all semester. More off than on, to be truthful. Things must be changing between us 'cause now he's asked little old me to the big campus Theta ball. A smile splits my lips just thinking how jealous the girls on the hall are going to be when they see him sporting me into that ball...but only if I lose some weight and look like *he* wants me to look.

Stefan has been working on "improving" me since I first arrived. I'm trying to be what he wants...but no matter how I change, it never seems enough. He told me that I needed to update my wardrobe, work on my hair and lose weight, so I did. I spent part of my scholarship money to buy some Tommy Hilfiger shirts—did you know they cost sixty dollars a piece?—got some fake nails, arched my eyebrows but, I drew the line at getting some blue colored contacts. I am *not* Lil' Kim.

Then, I went on the Cabbage diet. Nothing but cabbage, cabbage and more cabbage for fourteen days. I lost ten pounds the first week alone. I tell you I was ecstatic when Stefan started paying more attention to me, but I had to give it up because the gas was killing me *and* my roommate.

I moved on to the All Protein Diet. Now, this diet requires that you eat only meat. It worked too. I lost another ten pounds. Stefan was standing on his head, happy that I was about to become his "dream woman." I was too.

Pretty soon though, my body rebelled. An all-protein diet isn't healthy and my body let me know it. My kidney's hurt from trying to get rid of all the protein waste and I noticed that my sweat really smelled. Not funky but...I don't know, just *strange*. No matter how many showers I took, I still didn't smell fresh.

My roommate told me to get off that fool diet before I killed myself trying to please some boy. Even though I'd lost twenty pounds and Stefan said I was "da bomb," I knew she was right. So, I started eating like every other normal girl in college—anything fast food, fried and of course, Chinese.

The weight was back in a month and Stefan let me know it. He showed out something awful when I began wearing my "pre-weight loss" clothes again. Said I'd just let myself go all to hell. You'd think I was two hundred pounds instead of the one hundred forty I am. At five-four, that's not too bad. Most guys think I'm fine...that is except Stefan.

Walking over to the long mirror, I take a moment to survey myself. My skin is clear and chocolate as a Nestle's bar. Black hair, worn any which way I can arrange it to look decent in the morning, just reaches my shoulders. Medium-sized breasts (more than a handful is a waste, so they say) jut from my chest. Healthy thighs connected to a healthier behind complete the package. Turning sideways, I check out the nice protrusion of curvature attached to my lower spine and sigh. I truly have 'junk in my trunk.'

How in the world am I gonna lose twenty pounds in the next two weeks for Stefan?

Frustrated, I turn from the mirror and fling myself back amongst the clothes on my bed, not caring that I was squishing the navy linen pants suit I'd worn to the high school awards banquet back in May *and* which I just had cleaned.

The phone rings, interrupting my pity party.

I hurriedly stretch my hand out for the headset. Clearing my throat and swallowing quickly, I lower my voice seductively and say, "Huh-looo." *Never can tell when Stefan would be calling!*

"Sis? That you?" A squeaky male voice says into the phone.

"Weenie?" I ask. Weenie's the pet name for my 16-year-old brother, André Andrews III. He got the nickname from his penchant for hot-dogs. And when I say he like hot-dogs, that's an understatement. He can eat hot-dogs for breakfast, lunch, dinner, snack, brunch, holidays, etc. Shoot, the only thing I know he loves more than hot-dogs is gossip. He likes to hear it and he loves to pass it on, filling in any blanks that may be missing in the original telling, of course.

"Yeah. Whazzup? How's it going?"

"Pretty good. I'm just trying to find something to wear to a ball. What are y'all doing?" I ask as I settle the pillows behind my back while pulling the pantsuit from under my hips.

"Nothing. Shoot, you forgot where we live? What's to do?" Weenie's voice squeals out a high-pitched, shrilly and *familiar* complaint from him. He's always saying he can't wait to finish school, so he can go where the action is. Yokel, Mississippi— population minimus— just doesn't offer that. "Del, did Moma call you?"

I'm instantly on alert. "Ah…no. Is something wrong?"

"Not…really." I hear the hesitation in his voice.

"What's wrong, Weenie?" I sit up in the bed, alarmed.

7

"Well..." There was a bulk of untold meaning in that one word.

"What?!" I yell, anxiousness and frustration making me irritated that he couldn't just *tell* me.

His voice drops a notch, "Don't say nothing if Moma calls. Just act like you haven't heard a thing from me 'cause you know she like to be the first one—"

"Weenie, *what is it*?!" I cut him off.

"Well, Madame A is in the *hos*pital," Weenie says profoundly.

Madame A is the name our 75-year-old grandmother requested we call her. She said she didn't want to be no Big Moma, Grandmama or Muh'dear. Call her Madame A. 'So dignified sounding,' she told us.

"In the hospital?! What happened?" I ask, as scenes of my grandmother on a life support machine flashes through my mind. I bunch my shirt in my hand and hold it tight to my chest, fearful of what he will tell me next.

"Del, the old girl's still got it. Do you hear me? She's *still* got it! These women walking 'round here trying to be players need to take a lesson or two from that old girl."

What in the world is he talking about? "Weenie, if you don't tell me what happened, I'm going to..."

"Aw'ight. Aw'ight. This is what happened. Madame A, unbeknownst to us and the rest of the town, has two, I said not one, but *two* men friends."

"Stop it." What kind of mess is he talking about? He's got to be exaggerating.

"Girl, she's in a love triangle!"

"Quit lying!"

"I'm not! You 'member Mr. Suge Benson's son by Miz Easter Chaps, Fred?"

"Yeah." Miz Easter Chaps has been Madame A's nemesis for at least a hundred years. I not sure what the whole deal is, but I think it had something to do with her husband and Madame A.

"Well, he's been tipping over to see Madame A on the sly."

"You're kidding me! Mr. Fred's maybe... what...55 at the most! Madame A is *way* too old for him." Now if he was gonna exaggerate, he could have *at least* made it believable. Ain't no way Madame A was committing cradle robbery like this!

"Apparently not," Weenie says chuckling.

"Yeah, right. Who's supposed to be the other man?" I ask, expecting another unbelievable choice of men in town from him.

"Del, you're not gonna believe this here. You know old man Smithey Zacharias that use to run the newspaper?"

"Old *white* man Smithey Zacharias?"

"Yeah, old *white* man Smithey, you know any others?" Weenie says sarcastically.

"Don't you tell me he's the other one?!" I exclaim. I know this *can't* be true!

"Well, he is."

Are they going crazy down there?! Yokel, Mississippi must be about to have a riot!

"Uh uh. What in the world would Madame A be doing with a white man?"

"Now, you need to stop acting like she hadn't opened *that* door before." Weenie says peevishly.

"Yeah, but she wasn't in Yokel. Mr. *Zacharias*? He's got to be all of 70. Are you sure?"

"I don't have no eye-witness account, but they say old girl sure had him cutting up right there on Main Street. So it's safe to say she telling him *something*." I can hear the excitement in Weenie's voice as he relays this tidbit of juicy street trash.

Dog, Madame A's got two boyfriends that seem to be vying for her affections and I can't keep one happy. I don't stop myself from laughing, "What happened?" I finally manage to catch my breath and ask.

"Somehow, somebody got their wires crossed and both of the 'men friends' showed up to escort Madame A to brunch on Thursday after her Women's Club meeting."

"O...kay," I say slowly. I don't know what Madame A was doing up in the Women's Club Meeting anyway. She always said they were a bunch of dried-up, old hags trying to run the world like we were still back in "Jubilee" times. Always waiting for "The Man" to make the decisions and we react accordingly.

"Madame A decided that since the mistake was all hers, they should *all* go to brunch together."

"No!" I exclaim. Madame A can't be this bold!

"Yes. Well, neither of these cats knew *jack* about the other one. The way I heard it, they both looked mad, but neither one of them wanted to be the first walk away and let the other one escort her to brunch."

"So, what *happened*?"

"Stop interrupting and I'll tell you! Well, they each had an arm—Mr. Fred pulling her one way and old man Zacharias pulling the other—trying to get her to go towards each one of their cars. I guess whoever got her to ride was supposed to have a leg up on the other one. Anyway, they said they were pulling and pushing on her like an old mule stuck in mud."

"On Madame A?"

"Uh hum. Well, Del, they pulled and pushed until she slipped on a rock and fell flat on her back."

"Oh, no! She didn't break her hip, did she?" I ask with dread, knowing that it took old people a long time to heal broken hips.

"No, she didn't break her hip, but she broke her arm in two places and she has a bruised kidney."

I sigh, disgusted and concerned too. "How is she?"

"She's resting pretty good, but Moma is fit to be tied."

"What's new?" My mother, Lena Andrews, is Miss Prissy come alive. She lives in fear that somebody in the family will commit some transgression that will forever shame her.

"She was all scared when Miz June called to tell her they had taken Madame A to the hospital 'cause she fell. But when Moma found out *how* she fell, she showed out something awful at the hospital. Yelled at Madame A and all."

"I can picture that." Moma only worries about *others* transgressing, it's all right when she does it.

"Pissed Madame A off *bad*! Madame A told her and I quote, 'take your dry ass home and don't come back *until* I call for you. Ain't *nobody* asked you to be up in my business.'"

"Ohhhhhh! What did Moma do then?!" I yell. I *know* Lena Andrews didn't take that too well.

"She looked like she was gonna say something smart back, but the look Madame A had on her face must of stopped her. So, Moma snatched her purse off the chair and told me to come on. She didn't say another word until we got home."

"Where is she now?"

"Down there messing up Daddy's dinner yelling and crying about how bad Madame A treats her."

"She know you on the phone?"

"Noooo indeed! She'd take away my Playstation and telephone if she caught me!" Weenie gets quiet, then whispers, "Del, here comes somebody. Bye!" Click.

I place the phone back on the hook and look up at the ceiling. Madame A is a trip! Two men. *Younger* men at that. I laugh thinking about how they must've looked tugging on her and her standing there probably looking cool and collected as usual. The phone rings and breaks my thoughts.

"Huh-loo-ooo." I say in my sexiest hope-its-Stefan-calling voice.

"Delphine Andrews, is this how I taught you to answer the phone?" the stern voice of my mother asks me.

I ignore the question. "Hey, Moma, how you doing?"

"Terrible. Things are just a mess. A pure old D mess."

"What's wrong?" I try to interject some surprise in my voice since I already know why she's calling.

"It's your grandmother. She's still running around here acting like she's your age and got her arm broken."

"What happened? Is she all right?"

"What happened is that your grandmother's got man troubles bad. Somebody's gonna get their head cracked open if she don't watch it."

"Man troubles?"

"Yes. Your grandmother has taken up with two men and they got in a tussle over her and she fell and broke her arm. Can you believe this mess? A 75-year-old great-grandmother got men out in the street fighting over her! Main Street at that! It's a wonder somebody didn't get killed!"

"Moma, you sure they were fighting over her? Maybe she got in the way of a fight."

"Yeah, she got in the way, all right...Right in the *middle* of the whole mess. I can hardly hold my head up, I'm so ashamed at her." And the rest of the family too.

"Moma, you overreacting. I'm sure it was just a little misunderstanding and Madame A just happened to get in the middle of it."

"Oh. Now I'm *lying*?"

"No! Moma, I didn't say you were lying at all!" I'd rather *die* than call Lena Andrews a lie. I'll go to *hell* before I do that!

"Sounds like what you said. I tell you that my mother had two men fighting over her and you're saying that's not what happened. I'm here with the action and you're way up there at school and you're saying I didn't see and hear what I saw and heard? Now if that's not calling me a lie, then I don't know what is!" Moma was working herself up something awful!

"I'm sorry. I didn't mean to seem like I was calling you a lie. It's just that…Madame A with men fighting over her in the streets…"

"…is a durn mess! Then both of them showed up at the hospital at the same time. She needs to get them on a schedule. I told her so! Now, she's sitting up in the hospital acting like I did something to her. She talked to me like I was somebody else's child. Who she think gonna take care of her when she comes home? Maynard? Brenda? No! It's gonna be me! That's who." Maynard and Brenda are my mother's siblings. They are constantly at each other about something.

"Moma, just calm down. When's she supposed to get out?"

"The doctor said she should be in there maybe a week."

"Well, we've got Spring Vacation coming up, and since I'll be home, maybe I could stay with her during that time."

"I don't know. Mama can be a real handful. She's so damn hard-headed, I know I'll be pulling my hair out before the first day is through. Let me think about it and I'll let you know."

"That's sounds good."

"Well, baby, I'm gonna go back down and talk with you Daddy. He said he's got a touch of indigestion. I don't know if it was the hot sausage I messed up and put in the red beans and rice or what. Anyway, let me go check on him. Take care and I'll talk to you soon."

"All right Moma. Love you."

"Love you too. Bye."

Looks like Spring Break going to be a trip!

I hang up the phone with smile on my lips which is short-lived when I realize that Stefan hasn't called me today.

Not once.

I mentally try to will the phone to ring. When that doesn't work, I scream at it.

Nothing.

Finally, I retrieve the book from the floor and begin reading again. Hey, I've got a long way to go before I reach Stefan's level of perfection and time's wasting.

CHAPTER

2

Madame A.

Adoll Mackey. Well, she's Bernstein now. Her whole name is Adoll Trudy Mackey Smith Whitehead Berstein. A whirlwind on legs. She's managed to bury three husbands, and if what Weenie and Moma says is true, she might get another one before it's over.

Madame A puts the "E" in eccentric. She does what she wants, when she wants, how she wants and the hell with the rest of us. She's managed to make enemies with most of the women in Yokel since the men, young and old, all love to flirt with her. And she *loves* to flirt back. She likes nothing better than to be surrounded by men, and she usually is. A man magnet if there ever was one.

Four feet, eleven inches and rounded in not just the right places, but all over, my grandmother is a true testimony to the old adage *'you are only as old as you think you are.'* And I think my grandmother never got past 21. No long dresses and old hairstyles for her. She'll slap on a blond wig in a minute!

The last time I was home, Madame A had on capris and 3-inch heels. Moma told her she looked like she needed a corner to work. Madame A just patted her auburn, waterfall hairdo—yes, I said waterfall—and went on to the church picnic. It's gotten to the point, I don't know *who* she'll be when I get home.

I slow down as I pass the WELCOME TO YOKEL, MS HOME OF THE PIG'S FEET FESTIVAL POPULATION 1,876 sign. The last time I came home, I managed to get a ticket from my police-officer cousin, Donnell. I should have known better. He'd give his Moma a ticket.

Yokel is what folks from other parts of the country imagine the South to be—sleepy, slow-moving and divided straight along the color lines. Our high school still has two Homecoming Queens—one "ethnic" and one white, of course—two maids for each grade, and two of each Class Favorites. I don't know why they say "ethnic" 'cause the only ethnic people in town are black. Ain't no Hispanics, Asians or Native Americans around here. They could just say what they mean—black. I guess they're hoping somebody else will come up in here and give them some relief from our blackness.

I pass through the Main Street of the big downtown area. I'm being facetious when I say big—a

Stack & Sack grocery store, two gas stations that still pump gas for you, the Local Yokel newspaper office and a Bill's Dollar Store. Cars are lined up slant-wise between the yellow lines directly in front of the businesses. A smattering of smaller offices for the doctors and lawyers are located directly behind this street. The big castle-like hospital sits on a hill in the distance. *They must have had Snow White as the architect.* The only fast food places we have are the Tasty Freeze and Spunky's and we're on family terms, if you know what I mean.

I wave as I see Miz June, one of Madame A's oldest friends, her dress riding up, showing her knee-highs tied in a knot below her ashy knees, getting into a car. I beep my horn at my aunt, Brenda, as she pulls on a little girl I don't recognize with braids hanging down her back. Slowing down at the one yellow caution light in town, I turn down a Carver's Road, the two-lane, black-top road leading towards our house.

Letting the window down, the air flows in bringing the scents I know so well—cow manure and freshly turned earth. As I turn a curve, I see a few cows and calves milling in the center of the road and I slow to a crawl. My cousin, Binky, tore up his car when he hit a cow last year and I didn't want that to happen to me. No telling when I'd get another one. Blowing my horn loud and long, they shift and shuffle off to the side making way for me. Still, I creep past 'cause it's not unusual for a sow to be roaming loose around here and they can mess up a car just as bad.

Pulling into the driveway of our house, I see that both the car and truck are gone. Turning off the car, I can hear loud music, the bass thumping, as I get out. *Moma and Daddy are definitely not home if Weenie's playing his music this loud.*

Entering the house, I take a moment to absorb the scenes and smells of home—the tile floors with the flower patterns on them that my mother loves (and my father hates) flow from the den and over the rest of the house, the plaid, wooden-armed sofa that you can never get comfortable on and the worn LaZboy chair my father refuses to get rid of. The living room, reserved only for *important* company, is pristine as always, the furniture still covered in the original plastic from the factory. Wasn't no sitting on it just for fun either.

I loudly yell out, "I'm hoommme." Nobody answers so I continue to the back of the house towards the bedrooms.

The music is really loud as I walk down the hallway and a sickly-sweet smell assaults my nostrils. *What in the world is that?* The smell is a combination of musk, flowers and mothballs or something.

I pause at Weenie's door and both the music and smell drown my senses. Tapping lightly, I get no response so I throw open the door. Weenie is lying on his bed in his underwear, playing his video games with his back to the door. The funky smell is *definitely* coming from in here.

I stride over to him and pop him up sides the head. Weenie drops his game control and swings around, a wild look in his eyes.

Seeing me, he says, "Girl, don't be walking up on me like that!"

"Turn this music down!" I yell, hands on my hips.

Weenie saunters over to his stereo and slowly complies. Turning back to me, his face scrunched up in annoyance, he says, "Why you sneaking around the house? Daddy told you about that mess."

"Well, for your information, I wasn't sneaking. I called out when I first walked in the house and I knocked on your door. You should be glad I'm not Jeffrey Dahmer or your narrow behind would be in a butt lock right about now." I place my fist on either side of my hips and do some pelvic grinding.

"Ha. Ha. Jeffrey don't want *none* of this." Weenie points to his behind for emphasis. "Anyway, newsflash, Jeffrey Dahmer is dead."

"Yeah, but his buddies might not be. Where's Moma and Daddy?"

"Daddy's at work and Moma's over at Madame A's house."

"She at home already?"

"Naw. She's supposed to get out tomorrow. Moma is just over there tidying up."

"Oh." Moma always gonna keep herself moving. She's got to feel useful to somebody.

"Hey, I almost forgot, Moma told me to tell you when you get here, clean up the kitchen, sweep and mop the living room, family room and the bedrooms and to start dinner. She left the chicken she wants you to fry in the sink."

"Now who's the comedian? You know good and well Moma told *you* to do all that. When's she supposed to come back?"

"She just left about an hour ago, so I guess it will be a while."

As the central air kicks on and stirs up the sickly-sweet smell, I ask Weenie, "What *is* that awful smell in here?"

Looking confused, he asks me, "What? I don't smell nothing."

"You can't smell that sweet odor? It smells like a pimp's perfume or something."

"Oh, that. That's just this new cologne an old girl at school gave me. Men wear cologne, not perfume."

"She must hate you." *That stuff stinks.*

"*Who*? She wants some of me, that's why she gave it to me."

"Wants you for what? Ain't nothing there but bird-chest and butt."

"That's what you think. I got the girls all over me like buzzards on road-kill."

"Boy, you ain't got no game."

"Del, I'm *telling* you, I got more game than the Chicago Bulls had with Michael Jordan! You don't know *nothing* 'bout me." Weenie illustrates by hacking his hand just above the knee.

"In your dreams. In your dreams. I'm going over to Madame A's to see if I can help Moma out. You better get on the list she left for you or you're gonna be in *big* trouble."

Screwing his face up, he says, "Can you help a brother out? I've got stuff to do…"

"Get off the Gameboy and do them, then."

"This is a Playstation II. Don't be mixing them up again," he says, clarifying the difference to me, like I care.

"Whatever. Get on your chores or your behind will be in a head lock when Moma gets back." I throw my arms around my shoulder and act like I'm gasping for air.

"You are so funny. I'm calling 'Comic View' right now."

"Bye," I say as I leave out of the room.

I throw my bags into my bedroom and close the door. Getting into my car, I head back towards town and Madame A's house.

δ

Now Madame A's house is just as unconventional as she is. After her last husband died and left her a good bit of loot, she built a Spanish styled house complete with a tiled roof, a courtyard and a fountain out front. She said it reminded her of a "special place" she had spent some time. Moma told her she should build a nice brick ranch like everybody else had. Madame A told her that it was her money and she was gonna build whatever the *hell* she liked. She wasn't planning to leave her kids *squat!* She was gonna be living in their inheritance until she died. Moma didn't speak to her for three months after that.

I smile as I round the circular drive and approach the door. Moma's car is backed up near the front, the windows cracked, allowing the heat of the day to escape.

As I get out, chickens flow around the car, cackling loudly.

"Shoo," I say, "I don't have any bread for you guys."

I push past them, stepping carefully to avoid sinking my shoes into their droppings, as I walk along the stone pathway. I knock loudly and my mother answers quickly. A pink bandanna holds back her silver-sprinkled hair and she is wearing a long-sleeved shirt and some old pants. She'd look like she was in her 30's if she didn't have a permanent furrow dug into her forehead.

"Hey, Delphine," she says, enveloping me in a hug, "You just getting in?"

"A few minutes ago. I went by the house and Weenie said you were over here, so I came to see if I could help."

"I'm glad you came," she says as she ushers me into the house. "You've put on a little weight, haven't you?"

This pulls me up short—a positive comment to soften the negative criticism behind it. Classic Moma. "Uh, no. I don't think so." I stammer, trying to conceal the hurt I feel from her remark.

Stepping through the doorway, a smile lights my face as I survey the interior. Yellow and orange walls with a sunset and sunrise painted on them, greet me.

Clay pots overflowing with plants are lined along these walls. Shutters are hung on every window, no curtains in sight. Copper—bottomed pots hang along a wire across an island in the kitchen. A breeze picks up and the wind chimes on the patio call out longingly.

My mother misses the beauty of it all as she walks past me and says, "Come on. I was just cleaning up her bedroom."

I follow along, reluctant to leave the peacefulness I'd found. Walking down a red baked-tile hallway, we enter through a heavy wooden door and into her bedroom. A gigantic Spanish-styled iron bed with curling ironwork, the mosquito netting running to the floor, commands center stage. Huge pillows are everywhere.

"Have you ever seen any mess like this?" My mother asks, her furrow prominent in her face.

"You don't like it?"

"Who in the world would have a bed made out of junk iron in their room? And the pillows! I almost tripped and fell when I brought a load of laundry back here to put up."

"It's kind of nice. Funky." Madame A's room is phat!

"You're right it's *funky*. My Moma must have been out of her mind when they talked her into this mess."

I guess she didn't know I mean *funky* in a cool kind of way.

"I tell you somebody got over. Took an old woman's money, that's what they did."

Seeing that she and I *definitely* weren't on the same page, I say, "So, what do you need help with?"

"I'm gonna clean out this room. Let's see...we'll put all the pillows in the walk-in closet and...I'll tie that curtain around her bed back. Then we need to vacuum and I've got a nice cabbage print rug I bought to put on the floor. That should make the room at least presentable."

Cabbage print rug? Madame A is *truly* not the cabbage-print-rug type of woman. "Moma, you sure Madame A wants us to do this?"

"Del, I'm doing what's best for Moma. Ain't no way she can rest with all this *mess* around the room." Moma circles with her hands.

"Well...I think Madame A kind of likes this stuff and..."

"Now you listen here," Moma put her hands on her hips, "*I'm* the one who's got to navigate around this *junk* to help her and I don't plan to be up in here trying to break my neck every time she needs something. So you can either help me or go on back to the house. I don't want to hear another word about it."

I hold up my hands. "Let's just get on with it," I say, knowing that further conversation would be wasting my breath.

I slowly gather up the pillows and place them in the walk-in closet. My mother pulls the mosquito netting back and ties it around the bedposts. As I vacuumed the carpet, I almost gag when I see the *yougly* pink and yellow huge flower print rug my mother rolled out. *Madame A might just vomit when she sees her room.* My mother seems happy with the results though. The room is sterile, bearing no resemblance to the room we'd entered. I turned my back to block out the awful sight.

"What else we got to do?" I say a little sullenly.

"I need you to hang up her clothes, then we'll tackle the living room."

After pointing out the clothes, Moma goes into the front of the house. I can hear her grunting as she moves the big clay pots.

Walking into the closet, I snag my foot on a pillow and stumble. Falling forward, I try to catch myself by grabbing for the shelf and miss. A box dislodges its contents all over my head. Looking down, I realize that the floor is covered in photographs. Dropping the clothes in disgust, I lean over to pick up the photos.

The first photo I grab shows Madame A smiling widely into the camera, a dark-skinned man hugging her around the waist. I turn the black and white photo over and read the script writing, EDGAR AND ADOLL IN PARIS, 1950. This is my grandfather! I never knew him because he died way before I was born. They looked so happy together.

Picking up another photograph, I see Madame A lying facedown on a fur cover, completely naked, except for some material thrown over her hips. She smiles slyly into the camera, her eyes half-lidded and suggestive. *Madame A was hot!* Two more photos, obviously taken at the same time, show Madame A in other sexy poses.

I quickly pick up some more photos. Some show Madame A with my mother, aunt and uncle when they were little. Some had just her and my grandfather, Edgar, in them. Baby pictures of toothless kids are sprinkled throughout.

A picture of an older Madame A wrapped in the arms of an obviously white man, gives me pause. *Wonder who this is? It's definitely not old Grandpa Bernie.* Bernie Berstein was her last husband. The short, dark, balding Jewish man I remembered bore no resemblance to the tall, light-haired man in the photo.

"What do you think you are doing!" My mother suddenly yells in my ear while snatching the photos out of my hands.

I jumped a foot. "Ah…looking at some photos?"

"Well, you don't need to be looking, you need to be hanging clothes!" My mother quickly gathers up the remaining photos and shoves them back into the box. "I told you to hang up clothes, now look how wrinkled they are. What were you thinking, girl? Moma should have thrown out those old photos a long time ago."

Her movements are stiff and jerky. *What's wrong with her?* "I was just looking. They fell by accident—"

"You just forget what you saw! Probably some stuff to mess with your mind and ask questions that are better left alone."

"Well she did have a picture with some white man...and I know it wasn't Grandpa Bernie, so who—"

"Don't say another word! I've got a good mind to burn all those pictures up. Why she would want to keep pictures of her and her men, I just don't know."

Her men? For some reason, the implications of this statement made me bolder. "She had pictures of you and Uncle Maynard and Aunt Brenda and she even had some of Granddaddy Edgar."

"Delphine...just...forget about the pictures. They might make your grandmother sad if you bring them up. Just leave the past in the past."

My mother finishes hanging the clothes and takes my arm and leads me out of the closet. Closing the door firmly, she leans against it, weariness in her eyes.

31

"Woooooooo. Let's just finish here and get on home. I've got to call the hospital and find out what time we should check her out." Placing a false, bright smile on her lips, she says, "You run on home. I've just about got all the plants out on the patio. Anyway, I don't want to be here after sundown."

"Why? What happens after sundown?" I ask apprehensively, as visions of werewolves and Boogey men suddenly pop into my head.

"Nothing. Moma just won't put up any curtains and it scares me. Anybody could be out there looking in at us and we wouldn't know a thing. Just like white folks."

I, personally, liked the open look of no curtains, but I also knew my mother well enough not to say it to her. "If you think you've got it, I'll just go and help Weenie finish the chores and I'll see you at home." I turn to walk away.

"Del...thanks. Glad you're home." My mother calls after me.

"Yeah. Me too."

I slowly walk out to my car, resolving that at the first opportunity, I would ask Madame A. about those photographs.

$$\delta$$

Lena leans against the door as forgotten memories slam into her. She could see the playground like it was yesterday. The swings she loved, the sandbox, her friends, Lisa and Sandra giggling at her sand castle, then...

"*Lee Lee, your mama is a floozy.*" The dark face of Danny Ross springs out of her memory bank. He was a big, fourteen year old that lived in a broke-down house ten miles out of town with his parents and ten brothers and sisters. She hadn't thought about him or what he'd said on that playground in front of all of those kids in years.

"*Is not!*" *An eight-year-old Lena yells back.*

" *That's what my moma says. She said your mama is like a dog in heat!" he taunts her.*

"*That's a story! You take that back!*" *Lena indignantly screams causing Lisa and Sandra to drop their shovels and scramble out of the sandbox.*

"*You calling my mama a lie? My mama don't lie!" Danny is the one that's indignant now. "She said your mama is just trash dressed up in good clothes laying around with white folks for money! She even took some naked pictures showing her—*"

Lena is standing now, hands fisted. "You say another thing about my mama and I'm gonna—"

"What? Whatcho little butt gonna do?" Danny leans in close enough for her to see the tartar collected near his gum line before he pushes her in the chest.

Lena falls to the ground but anger makes her jump right up and tell him off as much as her eight-year-old mind can think of. "You telling stories! That's why you so ugly!" She sticks out her tongue. "My mama says y'all ain't nothing but low-class folks! That's why your mama breeds like a rabbit!"

His hands snatch at her pigtails; the pain bringing tears to her eyes. He leans back into her face, his breath sour. "Don't you never say nothin' 'bout my mama. She don't lie! Your mama is a hussy and your daddy is white!"

This made her madder than a cornered snake. "My daddy ain't white!"

"Then why you so high yella? Your mama is brown skinned and the man they say is your daddy was coal black. How else you think you got to be so yella?"

Lena didn't know but she knew she wasn't no white girl. She slapped him as hard as she could in frustration.

She never even saw the fist that knocked her out...

Lena shudders as she pulls her mind back to the present. Danny was long gone to Chicago along with the rest of his family but that day was forever seared in her mind. It didn't help that she had found those "naked" pictures he'd described when cleaning up her mama's room. It just made it all seem true. Now here were the photos again, opening up a can of fresh worms; making Del ask questions that shouldn't ever be asked. Want answers she would rather her mama take to her grave.

Why couldn't Mama get rid of that old mess?

Lena notices the sun getting lower and shivers. She pushes the memory down as locks the house tight before getting into her car.

CHAPTER

3

I awaken early the next morning. The gray of dawn is just peeking over the horizon; a rooster gives his natural wake-up call. I stretch lazily before getting out of bed. Looking out over the pasture, I throw up the window and inhale the fresh country air. The birds are twilling out love songs and the flowers bow from the dew.

I love this time of morning. Nobody's awake but me, nature and God. I sit a moment thanking God for another good day and I plan for it to be a good one, too. Madame A is coming home from the hospital and I haven't seen her since Christmas.

A door opens and I hear footsteps in the hallway. They continue past my door and on into the kitchen. Soon, I hear water running and pots banging. The smell of bacon wafts pass my nose in minutes. Straightening up my bed, I grab my robe and head for the kitchen.

My mother, her hair tied up in a bright scarf and wearing a new robe, is standing over the stove. The smoke from the hot skillet is being pulled out by the exhaust fan on the hood.

"Good morning," I call out cheerfully.

"Hey, baby. Sleep good?" My mother asks me.

"I always sleep good whenever I'm home. Must be the fresh air and all."

"Probably the lack of loud music and people coming and going all times of the day and night," she says with a snort.

"Yeah, probably that too." I chuckle.

"Wash up and wake your Daddy. He wants to get on the tractor early. Spring planting is just around the corner."

The same familiar cycle—disk up the ground, plant the seeds, spray the herbicide and harvest the crop. Year after year. Since time began.

"Sure." I retrace my step to the large master bedroom in the back of the house. I knock quietly and a gruff voice calls out, "Come in!"

Peeping around the door jam, I see my father sitting on the side of the bed rubbing his face and neck. Seeing me he says, "Hey, Del. Sorry I didn't get in before you went to bed last night." My father is a tall, wiry, cream-colored man. A foreman up at the tire plant in Natchez ever since I can remember, my father always left early and came home late. Well it seemed late to me.

Moma was always putting a plate in the oven for him because he was rarely home for dinner. Gray is sporting at his temples, but it only enhances his handsomeness. Right now, the sleep monkeys have written all over his face and it is full of lines and squiggles from the sheets.

I rush over to hug him. "Good morning, Daddy. Moma says get up 'cause you want to get an early start on the plowing," I say as I settle myself besides him on the bed.

"Did she now? Seems like she always gets me up at the crack of dawn, on my *day off*, when I need to do something around the house," he says, chuckling.

"Oh, Daddy."

"Well she does."

"I guess she's just getting you started early since she has to leave early to see about Madame A."

A grimace mars his smooth features. "Your Moma needs to let her brother or sister handle Ms. Doll. All they gonna do is fight, fight, fight. Them two women gonna kill each other before it's over."

"They are not. All mothers and daughters have disagreements."

"Really. How many daughters you got?"

"None, but I *am* a daughter and me and Moma always disagree about something. That's the nature of the relationship."

"Nature of the relationship? That something you learn up there at school?"

"Yep. Psychology 101, Chapter 3. 'Family Relationships And Interactions.' You see, mother-daughter relationships are oftentimes complex. There is a need for every mother to want to see themselves mirrored in their daughters. Now this is the exact opposite of the actions they want to see in their sons. Mothers want their sons to be—"

"Stop. Please." My father holds up his hands. "It's too early for me to be in class. Tell your Moma I'll be there in a minute."

"All right, Daddy. See you in a few." I kiss his cheek and rise from the bed.

"Del?"

"Yes?"

"Tell Weenie to get up. I'm gonna need him with me today."

"Sure thing, Daddy. Bye."

Walking back up the hall, I knock loudly on Weenie's door. Hearing muffled mumbling, I open the door and flip on the overhead light. Seeing the lump in the middle of the bed, I roughly snatch the covers from the form underneath.

"What?!" Weenie shoots up from the bed. "Turn the light off! Can't you see I'm trying to get some sleep?" His hands grab for the bedspread.

"Daddy says to get up. He needs you to be ready to go to the field with him in a little while."

"Awww….I don't want to go to the fields today." He says with a groan.

"So? You better get your butt up, much as you eat."

"I'm sick and tired of going out to the fields. Why can't we buy all our food like everybody else does?" He whines.

"You know why." Ever since it was rumored that the fruit and vegetables from Mexico had pesticides which harmed the development of children sprayed all over them, my mother has been adamant about growing her own. If *anybody* was gonna poison her children, it was going to be her. I admit that a two-acre garden is a bit much, but what my mother wants, she usually gets.

"Shoot."

"It could be worse. Moma might hear that they're trying to poison the meat supply then you would have to raise some cows and pigs too."

Holding his head in his hands, Weenie says, "It's the 21st century and we still living like *Little House on the Prairie*."

"Well, get up Little Joe, there's work to be done."

"That's *Bonanza*."

"Oh. Well, get up Laura."

"You still funny. Get out."

"Moma almost has breakfast done. You better get up before I eat it all. We ain't cooking no more."

"I'll be there in a few, aw'ight?" Weenie says, collapsing back on the bed, the cover held in his fists.

"Remember what I said!"

His reply was muffled beneath the covers. Returning to the kitchen, my mother sets a plate of bacon and eggs on the table and pushes a strand of hair back under her scarf.

"Del, stir the grits so they won't burn. I've got to get dressed if I want to be there when they release Moma."

"What time is she supposed to get out?"

"The doctors said around 8:30. We definitely have to have her out by 9:00 or they will bill us for another day."

"I'll be over just as soon as I get dressed."

"No need to hurry. I want you to bake some chicken for your Daddy and brother to eat for lunch. It's in the refrigerator next to the butterbeans you need to go ahead and put on. Oh, don't forget to make some cornbread to go along with it." Looking around the kitchen, making sure she didn't miss any new chores for me, she says, "I guess that's it. I'm gonna wash up and head on out."

"Aren't you gonna eat something first?"

"No, baby, I'm not too hungry. I'm just ready to pick up Mama and get her settled. I imagine that might take more time than expected as fussy as she gets sometimes."

"I'll come over just as soon as I get everything cooked and ready."

"That will be fine. Remember to cook the butterbeans on medium heat and don't forget to put more meal than flour in the cornbread. You are *not* baking a cake."

"I remember, Moma." *Will she please go and get dressed?*

As she leaves the room, I grab a plate and fill it high. No low-fat food up in here! The fresh eggs and bacon make my taste buds slap the top of my mouth with the first bite. Savoring the taste, I try to slow the chewing motion of my mouth, but I find myself unable to gain voluntary control.

How you gonna lose weight eating like this? my inner voice intrudes.

I will the voice silent as I inhale three toasts, some eggs, bacon and half a plate of grits before my father makes his entrance into the room.

Seeing me sopping up the last of my grits with my toast, he asks, "Leave any for me?" My jaws are puffed out, so I nod my head and point to the stove. "Girl, don't they give y'all breakfast up there at school?" I nod my head again. "Can't tell."

Swallowing and finding my voice, I reply, "It's not the same. The eggs are powdered and runny; the bacon is usually cold and fried too hard, so all I get are pieces; the toast don't have any butter on them; and they act like they don't know what grits are."

"If the food's so bad, why don't you come home more often? The way you stay up there, I thought they had a gourmet chef cooking y'all's meals."

"I wish."

My mother swishes through the kitchen on her way to the car. "See you guys later. Del's fixing lunch, so come in to eat a little before noon."

Kissing my father on the cheek, he pats her behind and she admonishes him with, "Quit! You see Del up in here!"

"And?"

"You *know* you know better!"

"Go on and get your Mama before I take you in the back room and release some of your stress again like I did last night. Del, you should have seen your Mama. She was—"

"Stop it!" My mother yells, her hands splayed across his mouth. "Del, don't listen to anything your Daddy said and remember to get the food on."

Snuggling her close, my father tells her, "You get your Mama settled and come on back home now. Let Maynard and Brenda do something for once."

Disbelief crosses Moma's face, "You get a brain transplant or did I get new siblings?"

"Just remember I'm waiting on you, woman."

"Bye. Have a good one."

"Love you, baby."

"Love you, too. See you, Del."

"See you in a little bit, Moma."

Watching her walk out to the car, my father turns to me and says, "It's a wonder we managed to get you and your brother, the way she acts. Everybody knows married people mess the sheets up every now and then."

Stunned that he would reveal this much of their personal life to me, I mumble, "Okay."

"Shut your mouth and eat. Call Weenie again 'cause it don't look like you plan to leave him anything."

"Will do. Weeeennnniiiieeee!" I yell at the top of my lungs.

"Girl, I could have done that. Go *get* him."

Sauntering down the hall, I can barely wait to get lunch finished and head over to see Madame A.

CHAPTER

4

Stirring the butterbeans over the hot stove, I hum to myself. The chicken is baking, the beans are on the stove and I managed to make a pan of cornbread that resembled cornbread, not muffins. Pushing a strand from my forehead, I wish for the millionth time that somehow you could cook a meal and not make the kitchen hot as Hell.

I've been cooking since I was about five. It makes me laugh when the guys I know are always lamenting about how there are no girls that are "real women" like their Momas. Shoot! Most of their Moma's held jobs and came home and continued working—cooking, cleaning and helping with homework. That ain't no dream life. I can cook and clean with the best of them. I just don't want to do it.

Cutting off the stove and placing the cornbread in the oven with the chicken, I pat my face with a paper towel and grab my car keys. Walking towards my car, I wave at Weenie as he plods towards the fence on the tractor, the wide brim of his hat shielding him from the hot rays of the sun. I promise myself that I'm gonna walk around the pasture and get some exercise later on that day before I hop into my car.

I whistle off-key as I drive along the road. Madame A is finally at home. Now, if I can just get her alone, I can ask her about the photos. Moma's gonna be mad, but as much life as Madame A's lived, I don't believe she would mind telling me about it.

Pulling up into the drive, I inhale the sweet smell of the wildflowers peeking their buds towards God. I park and avoid the chickens as I walk to the door. Tapping lightly, I'm surprised to see it opened by my grandmother.

Petite, with full facial makeup, Madame A is dressed fashionably as always, wearing gauchos with a matching top. Time has been good to her—face barely lined with wrinkles, giving her character, and pooling black eyes that have a generation of knowledge in their depths. She has a casted arm in a sling and the other one she holds wide. "Come here, baby. It's been a few months of Sundays since I've seen your pretty face."

"Hey, Madame A. Where's Moma? Shouldn't you be lying down or something?" I ask, coming into her embrace.

Snorting, she says, "I laid in that bed for more than a week. They don't seem to remember that I broke my arm, not my leg. Your Mama is putting away the luggage. We just walked in the door."

"Does Moma know you're out here?"

"So what if she does? This is my house. She can leave any time she gets ready. I can hire somebody to help me up in here. She don't have to stay."

"You know she wants to help out."

"Ain't stopped Maynard and Brenda from coming by, now did it?"

"They came by?"

"No, just wanting to help out hadn't made them come by. I guess they're thinking about me in their hearts," she snorts.

"I'm sure they will be here shortly."

"Girl, if you're gonna lie to somebody, don't let it be yourself. I raised each of them and I'm telling you, unless somebody tells Maynard or Brenda I'm dead, they ain't coming by today," she says this matter-of-factly.

"Well, at least you've got me and Moma."

"Yes, I do. Now come on in here and tell me about school. I know you've got yourself a young man. What's his name?"

Giggling, I say, "I don't really have a boyfriend, I just have a male friend. His name's Stefan."

"Male friend? What's this mess about? You young girls selling yourselves short letting these jokers 'test the waters' and not commit to anything in return. Men need guidance. Let them do anything with you and anybody else they want and they damn near lose their minds."

"Well..." I begin, feeling abashed.

"Get somebody you can tell the world he is your boyfriend. Let them male friends be just that—male friends. If they want to act like they're still in elementary school, then let them find an elementary school-minded girl."

"Yes ma'am," I answer properly. *Madame A doesn't understand anything about college, does she?*

"Now, what else you been up to? I see they're feeding you good. You've finally filling out. Keep it up and you're gonna turn more head than I did when I was your age."

"Now, Mama, if Del keeps on filling out ain't nobody gonna want her," my mother comments, walking into the room, echoing my unexpressed fears.

"Lena, why'd you go and say something like that? Ain't nothing wrong with Del." Turning to me, she says, "Del, always find somebody who wants the real you. Don't walk around trying to suck in your stomach or wear a girdle and all. Look for somebody who appreciates your

49

body how it is, not how they imagine it is. Don't try to sell what you ain't got in stock!"

"Mama, don't nobody want no big woman!" my mother persists, her face wrinkled up, forcing her furrow to become prominent in her face.

I know it. Why you got to say it?

"You better turn on *Oprah* sometimes. Big women are the rage. A man wants a woman he can *feel*, if you know what I mean." Madame A finishes with a wink.

"Yes, Madame A." I reply, knowing that she is really just trying to make me feel good about my size.

My mother completely changes the conversation. "Mama, don't you think you should lie down? Your room is all ready for you. Me and Del rearranged everything so you don't trip over anything."

I can tell by the way Madame A's back stiffened that this was trouble. "Lena, don't tell me you done messed with my room."

"We just got some of that...stuff up out of the way."

"Hmmph. Let me see what suburban interior decorating y'all have done."

Walking slowly to her room, she runs her hands over the countertop and down the wall of the hall. Pausing at her bedroom, I see her shaking her head.

"Where is all of my stuff?" Madame A finally growls out.

"You don't like it?" my mother asks incredulously.

"Lena, who did you think you were bringing home? Martha Stewart?" Madame A absolutely, positively hates anything like that. She said that if she was supposed to live amongst stuffed and frilly things, then God would have made her into a plush animal.

"Mama, all we did was put away the pillows and place a new rug on the floor," Moma tells her, exasperation tingeing her voice.

"I see what y'all did, I'm just wondering who you did it for?"

"Mama, those pillows were all in the way. You could have tripped over them and broken your other arm and that netting could have made you slip getting out of the bed."

"It hadn't made me slip in all this time and I like those pillows. It makes me feel like I'm living in a place I once visited."

"I was just doing it for your own good." My mother crosses her arms.

"I know what's good for me. I want my pillows back and the netting down. And for Heaven's sake, take that 1970's rug with you when you leave." Madame A points to the rug like she was putting a curse on it.

"I knew it was a mistake trying to help out," my mother says, her face pinched.

"Lena, now you wait just one minute. I appreciate you trying to help me out. I just like my own stuff and I want to surrounded by things that comfort me. I'm too old to be putting up with any old mess just 'cause *you* think I should like it. You know that."

"But—"

"Nothing. You go on home. You got your husband and children to think about. I'll be find up in here by myself."

"No, indeed not! I'm not letting you stay here by yourself," Moma protests.

"I've *been* staying by myself," Madame A retorts.

"You didn't have a broke arm then," Moma counters.

Sighing, Madame A says, "If it would make you feel better, why don't you let Del stay and help me out. We haven't spent much time together in a long while. We can catch up and she can do the things I might need doing."

"Well…"

"Oh, Moma, please?" I implore her, my hands clasped together like I was about to pray. "I would *love* to help Madame A."

"Mama, I don't think—"

"Hush now, Lena. Del says she wants to stay and I want her to stay, so that's that."

"You sure?"

"I'm positive. I'm not gonna eat her, you know," Madame A finishes with a chuckle. "Go home and let Del stay."

"All right, if you think you will be fine with just her here, I'll let her stay."

"Yes!" I yell.

"Shoo. Check on Andy and Weenie. They're probably missing you." She waves her hand to get Moma moving.

"Well, I'll be going then. Oh, Del, I left some chicken breasts in the sink. I thought Mama might want something to eat a little later. You should probably bake—"

"Forget those breasts. Me and Del are going into Natchez to eat," Madame A smirks.

My mother stops and turns back. "I don't think you should be out of the house so soon, Mama."

"Girl, I just broke my arm, I didn't have no baby."

"You still need to rest," Moma insists.

"And I'll get some rest," Madame A placates her, "I just want to take my granddaughter out to lunch. What's wrong with that?"

"Going out to lunch is what go you in this *mess* in the first place." Moma places her hands on her hips.

Madame A mimics her before replying. "No, some men starving for my company got me here."

"Mama, I've been meaning to ask you…what are you going to do about those two men? You aren't gonna keep seeing both of them, are you? Why, that's not right and somebody gonna get—"

"Bye, Lena." Madame A hands Moma her keys, "See you soon." Ushering her quickly to the door, she closes it just as Moma's butt clears the threshold. Leaning back on the door, she is quiet until she hears Moma's car leaving the drive.

"Chile, I feel like singing 'Hey, Ho, the wicked witch is dead' or something. Lena acts like I'm the child and she's the mother." Chuckling, she says, "Let's you and me get out of here before she comes back for something."

Grabbing the hand she offers, we quickly load into the car for the short drive to Natchez.

CHAPTER

5

We make general conversation on the drive to Natchez. As we head towards the river, Madame A remarks on the beauty of the historic homes along the streets. Slowing down for a buggy to pass, I ask if she wants to take a carriage ride and see the sights up close.

"No, baby. I just like riding and looking. Besides, our ancestors already know everything about every one of them houses since they built them all."

Navigating the tricky, one-way streets carefully, I manage to get the car to the restaurant in one piece. BUGLES AND BANJO'S is an eatery owned by one of Madame A's few women friends—Pearl Zealopala. An eccentric like Madame A, Ms. Pearl wears hot pink lipstick, bright necklaces and long skirts with fringe along the edges. She lives in a small, restored home on Wall Street. I once asked Ms. Pearl what nationality her name was and she told me American.

"I was born in America and my husband was too, so Zealopala is an American name. You know, you didn't have to arrive on the Mayflower to be an American," she said in stern tones.

Helping Madame A out of the car, we walk quickly to the restaurant's entrance. Spotting us as we enter, Ms. Pearl walks through the crowded dining area and greets us personally. She is dressed in a loud yellow skirt with an African patterned brown blouse. Dangling earrings and bangles finish the ensemble.

"My favorite girl! How you doing, Doll? And yes, I heard about the commotion you created up there in Yokel. You should be *ashamed* of yourself! Old as you are and still got the beaus acting a monkey for your old behind." She kisses Madame A on the cheek. "And who have you got with you? I know this isn't little Delphine, is it? Girl, I haven't seen you since you were knee high to a June bug. You all growed up now! Better watch out Doll, she gonna make the boys dig a trench in the road trying to get to the house to see her."

"She *is* a pretty thing, isn't she?" Madame A asks, proud admiration showing on her face.

"Sho' is. Y'all come on to the back. I've got a clear table overlooking the river. My special today is chitterlings served with onions, black-eyed peas, cornbread and blackberry cobbler or you can order something else from the menu." Passing us two menus from a side table, she says, "Order whatever you want. It's on the house."

Loud clattering from behind the closed doors leading to the kitchen makes her head turn sharply. "I'll be back. Let me see what these fools are doing back there."

Leaning forward, I ask Madame A, "You aren't eating chitterlings, are you?"

"Of course I am! Why, Pearl makes the best chitlins in town. You don't ever have to worry that somebody forgot to get all the fat and mess out of them. They are always clean and delicious."

Making a face at the thought of chitterlings, I tell her, "I'm ordering from the menu."

"I see Lena's still not letting y'all eat chitlins. Your Moma ate plenty when she lived with me. Well, chitlins, hog maws, pig's feet and pig's snout got us a long way. I love 'em!"

"I never ate them and...and I don't think I want to start today."

"Eat what you want. Pearl makes some good barbecue as well as fried chicken and pork chops."

Perusing the menu, I finally settle on some fried oysters. *It won't help my diet, but I can't eat them raw, can I? Besides everything else is loaded with calories. This is the lesser of the two evils.*

"Fried oysters?" Madame A says incredulously. "Now, you can't eat chitlins but you can eat some oysters? *Talk* about nasty. I once had a man tell me that oysters would get me 'in the mood.' I let him slide a slimy, raw one down my throat and it make me puke all over his suit and shoes." Shaking her head, she continues, "I've never had anything so *foul* tasting before in my life. The only 'mood' I got in was a bad one. No more oysters for me."

Laughing at her story, I could visualize the snit Madame A must have thrown after that. Looking over the crowded dining room done in Southern Comfort style, I say, "I see that Ms. Pearl is still packing them in. I would have thought she would be tired of cooking after all these years."

"What's to be tired of? Pearl's got five children. Before her man left her, all she did was cook all day. It's all she knows."

"Where did you and Ms. Pearl meet again?"

Staring out over the muddy waters of the Mississippi, a multitude of emotions pass across Madame A's face before she says, "Pearl got down on some hard times after her man left her with all them kids. I heard around town about this woman who was just walking the streets, begging for any little handout she could get. I got so sick about it, I walked around until I found her. You should have seen her—dirty hair and clothes; her face stained with tear tracks—I could have found that man that left her and shot him dead on the spot! Instead, I offered her a job at my folks' house. She helped my mama around the house and baby-sat your mother, uncle and aunt while I worked at the print shop."

"When did she decide to open up a restaurant?"

"About twenty years ago. She had long ago finished working for me and her kids were out of the house, all except the one that's a little slow, and she came to me and asked me how to get into business. Since she said all she knew how to do was cook and clean and she didn't want to clean none of the women's houses in town, I suggested she open a cafeteria. I gave Pearl a good bit of my savings and a big prayer. Combined with her prayers and hard work, this restaurant was born. Pearl paid me back in six months time." Madame A smiles as she relates this information.

"Wow. Ms. Pearl has been through some stuff!"

"Yes, she has. You girls today don't know nothing about hard times. You can be anything you want to be. Back then, we relied on men for everything. Be thankful you got the choices you got."

"I am, Madame A, I am."

Ms. Pearl returns with two platters heaped with food. Placing the chitterlings in front of Madame A, she says with a chuckle, "Do I need to cut up your food or get you a bib, Doll?"

"My arm's broke, not amputated. Just get me some extra napkins and I'll be fine."

"Sure I don't need to feed you? Now I don't mind helping out a friend—"

"Hush up! I ain't no invalid. Give Del her food before I call the Better Business Bureau and make a complaint," Madame A banters good-naturedly.

"Now it won't do you a bit of good if you did. You know all them Chamber of Commerce people eat here every day. They wouldn't believe a word you said against me," Pearl says smugly.

Setting my platter in front of me, she makes a quick exit. I inhale the tangy odor of the fried oysters.

"Girl, stop it. You about to make me ill with all that sniffing and stuff. Keep that platter on your side of the table. I don't want them oysters to accidentally touch my chitlins and make them nasty." Madame A's nose wrinkles up.

Oysters making chitterlings nasty? Right.

We eat in companionable silence, the click of the silverware interrupted only by our low moans of contentment. Finishing only half the platter of oysters, I lay my napkin down.

"Through?" Madame A asks, as she lifts another forkful of chitterlings to her waiting lips.

"I'm full as a tick. I think I'll ask them to put this in a doggy bag for me." I lie slightly. *I ate like a pig this morning. I've got to get this weight off or Stefan might try to take somebody else to the Theta ball and this food isn't helping one bit.*

"Uh hum," she answers, her mouth full to the brim.

Seeing that she is in good spirits, a nagging voice prompts me to ask about the photos I saw. Broaching the subject slowly, I remark, "Madame A, when we were cleaning up, or messing up, your room, a box of pictures fell down."

The fork stops midway to her mouth. Looking at me strangely, she motions for me to continue.

"I...I saw some of them with you and Grandpa Edgar, and Moma and Uncle Maynard and Aunt Brenda."

"Yeah..."

"I liked the ones where you were lying on the fur. I didn't know they let you take pictures like that back then."

Laughing loudly, she says, "Girl, you're a hoot! You can take any kind of pictures you want, if you got a camera. Besides, who do you think took those pictures?" Her eyes are twinkling.

"I don't know… I guess you had them made at a professional photographers, like those Fantasy Pose pictures they have now." I reply.

"Fantasy Pose? Del, they didn't have no Fantasy Pose back then. Your granddaddy took those pictures when we went to Brazil."

"He did?" *I wonder what other kind of pictures she took?*

"Yes indeedy. Edgar told me he wanted something 'special' to remember our time down there. It was a good time, too. I believe I conceived your Moma on that trip."

"Wow! Grandpa Edgar sounds like he was just as unconventional as you are."

"He was, God rest his soul. They just don't make them like him anymore. I tried two more times to find somebody like him. I got close, but they just ain't out there for me anymore. Oh well." I could see a mist forming in the corners of her eyes.

"Tell me more about him. Where did y'all hook up?"

"Well, I *met* your grandfather at a church service. I must have been about fifteen at the time. My Daddy had just got a new Ford truck and I had to ride on the back with my other sisters and brothers. The wind just whipped my hair all over my head. Now you got to remember, this was back in the early forties. We didn't get no perms at age two like the folks give girls today. I had my hair in two plaits like an Indian princess."

"Dag!" *Country with a capital C!*

"Well, there I was with my hair flying from all the wind, and I hear a voice asking me if they could help me down from the truck. I turned around and there he stood, wearing a suit at least two sizes too big and some scuffed boots on his feet. I wondered to myself who this clown was."

"You thought he looked like a clown?" I ask, confused.

"Not really, that's just the way we talked back then. Anyway, I tell him I don't need any help and I commenced to jump down and twisted my ankle on a rock."

"Oh no!" It seems like girl always do something crazy when they are trying to ignore a boy.

"He caught me and I swear, when he touched me, I could see a halo around his head. I was scared speechless! I thought he was a death angel about to take me away from there. I started hollering and bawling something *awful*!"

"Then what happened?"

"My Daddy comes over and shoves him to the side and asks me what he did to me. Of course he hadn't done a thing, so I just looked at my Daddy and babbled like a crazy mental patient. My daddy grabbed Edgar by the collar and shook him and demanded that he tell him what he did to me." Madame A demonstrates the shaking as well as she can with one good hand.

"I'll bet Grandpa was scared to death," I muse.

"No he wasn't. He just let my daddy shake him until he calmed down. Then he looked my daddy straight in the eyes and said, 'Sir, I was just helping my future wife. She twisted her ankle trying to jump out of the truck.' My daddy stared from him to me, then he just started laughing and walked off into the church."

"He just left y'all there?" I ask, surprised.

"Yep. I asked Edgar who he was and what did he mean by telling my daddy some mess like that. He introduced himself to me and told me he had been praying for a wife and that he'd had a dream that told him to go to this particular church and his wife would arrive on a truck. Now I wasn't the only girl on the truck, so I couldn't see how he figured I was the one. He told me that in the dream, the girl would ignore his help and he would be accosted by one of her family members. Since it all happened like the dream foretold, I, obviously, was his future wife."

"Get out!" *Talk about love at first sight!*

"I went in the church and left him standing there. That didn't stop your granddaddy, though. He came in and sat besides me, sharing his hymnal and bible throughout the service. I couldn't get rid of him after that."

"So when did y'all get married?"

"Well, he said that since he was 24, he expected his future wife to be a little older, but he was willing to wait a few more years until I was ready to leave the house."

"So you had to wait three more years?" *That is definitely a long time to date somebody.*

"No, we didn't last that long. Edgar got a scholarship to go to school up at Fisk and he asked my daddy for my hand before he left. I was tired of living with my parents and the never-ending farm chores. I wanted to see what was outside of Yokel, MS, so I married him."

"Just like that?"

"Just like that. Shoot, I could see that my mother and father weren't gonna let me out of their sights any time soon, so I decided I wanted to leave and see the big world out there."

"How was it?"

"Nashville was a big shock! I had never seen traffic like that! All we had in Yokel was a few trucks and horses and buggies. I got lost trying to get some groceries the first day! Soon, though, I started finding my way around and I settled into life in Nashville. When I got bored cleaning and cooking all the time, I applied for a scholarship and got accepted at Meharry's nursing school."

"What did granddaddy say about that?" I know he didn't like that one bit.

"He supported me! He wasn't like the other men back during that time. He told me to get all the schooling I could get and if they were going to pay for it, do it!"

"I didn't know you had a nursing degree, Madame A," I say, surprised.

"I don't. I got pregnant with Maynard after my third semester. Morning sickness and all made me drop out. By the time Edgar had finished, I didn't want to wait around and stay there just for school. See, Edgar had an opportunity to work with *World Life* magazine and they wanted to station him in Paris. Now this was a really good opportunity for a colored man, so I couldn't just hold him back trying to get my degree. We left out of there on the first ship sailing to England, yes we did." Madame A nods her head.

"Uncle Maynard was born by then?"

"Yep. We bundled ole Maynard up and took him with us. My Moma and Daddy were beside themselves.

They had never been on a ship, but they'd heard about the Titanic, so they were scared for us. They tried to talk us out of going or to leave Maynard with them at least, but we weren't hearing any of that. We just packed up all of our stuff and rode on down to New Orleans and got on a ship."

"What is Paris like?" I ask dreamily. Everybody always wants to go to Paris at least once.

"Y'all finished?" the voice of Pearl interrupts us.

"Almost. I was just telling Del about her granddaddy," Madame A answers.

"That's nice. I never met him Del, but the way your grandmother talked about him all the time, I feel like I did. Y'all need anything else?" Pearl inquires.

"Could I please have a container for the leftovers?" I ask. *I don't want her to think anything's wrong with the food.*

"Sure thing, baby. Let me get one for you." Retrieving the container quickly, she says, "Doll, now don't be no stranger. I live in the same house on the same street I've been living on the past 15 years. Stop by one Sunday."

"Will do, Pearl. Help me get my old bones out of this booth." Carefully watching the casted arm, Ms. Pearl gingerly helps Madame A to her feet. Placing her purse on the good shoulder, Madame A pats Pearl's arm and begins walking towards the door.

"See you, Pearl."

"Y'all come back now."

Arranging her in the car takes a little time. As I close the door, Madame A says, "I'm gonna grab a nap, Del. Wake me up when we get home."

I guess the remainder of the love story will have to wait, won't it?

CHAPTER

6

An unfamiliar, late-model truck is parked in the circular drive when we reached home. A man, sitting on the tailgate peeling an apple with a knife, rises as I slow the car to a halt. Tall, balding and thin all over, except for his "expectant mother" abdomen, a smile splits his lips as he sees us.

I shake my grandmother awake. "Madame A, a man is waiting for us. Do you know him?" He looks familiar, but I eye him suspiciously and keep the car running, just in case.

Rousing herself, she shuffles her body in the seat and yawns widely before focusing on what I'd just said.

"What?"

"A man is here. Look outside your window. Do you know him?"

Glancing out the side window, Madame A's face also splits into a smile. The man, apparently encouraged, walks to the door and opens it.

Patting her hair before she speaks, she holds out her good hand. "Well, if it isn't Fred Chaps in the flesh. What're you doing all the way out here?" Madame A says, voice light.

So this is Fred Chaps. I kinda remember him from when I was younger, but I don't know why. I'll bet his mama was fit to be tied when she heard about him and Madame A. First her husband, now her son.

"Doll, you knew I was gonna come and check up on my favorite girl," Mr. Fred says as he helps Madame A out of the car, pulling her into his embrace. "How you doing? I'm not hurting you, am I?"

"I'm doing fine, Fred, and no you aren't hurting me one bit."

"Doll, about the other day. I feel so bad about what happened and I want you to know I wouldn't do anything in the world to hurt you. That damn Smithey...'cuse my language, little lady..." he says to me, "that Smithey should have let go of you. He knew I was there first. He should have done the honorable thing and let me escort you."

Madame A pats his arm. "That's all right Fred. The mistake was all mine anyway. You had dinner?"

"Yeah. My baby girl celebrated her first anniversary so everybody was over there today."

"You coming in?"

"If you let me..." Mr. Fred stares into her eyes, pleading silently.

"You know I will. Come on then. Oh....Fred this is my granddaughter, Delphine. I think you might remember her."

"I haven't seen you since you were a little thing. Now look at you. Time sure goes fast," he says, nodding at me.

"Del, Fred owns the pharmacy over in Fayette. We've been doing business with him for many years, haven't we?"

"You and your whole family. I appreciate the support, too." Turning back to look in the car, he asks, "Doll, you got any packages I need to take in the house for you?"

"Naw. We've been over in Natchez eating at Pearl's place. Fred, she fixes chitlins that will make your see the Holy Ghost. The next time we go to dinner, I got to take you there."

"Fine with me." Placing a hand under her elbow, he helps her walk to the door. Extracting the keys from her hands, he opens it quickly.

I stand there watching them. My grandmother acts like she's my age with all that flirting and giggling. Mr. Fred is closer to sixty than fifty, but I can see he's already wrapped up in her mesmerizing web. What *is* it about her?

I follow them into the house at a leisurely pace, giving them plenty of room for any kisses they might not want me to see. Heck, I didn't *want* to see it. Slow murmuring, followed by giggles, reaches me as I enter the door. They stop and look up, guiltily, as I walk in.

"Baby, would you fix Fred some of that iced tea your Moma made? It's in the door of the Frigidaire." Madame A says, her good arm still intertwined in Mr. Fred's.

"Yes ma'am." I reach for a clean glass. As I collect the ice, I see Mr. Fred settling Madame A on the couch. Walking across the room, he stops at the ancient stereo and begins shifting through the LP's on top.

"It should be up there near the top. I listened to them just last week. Try the black cover…there it is. Put it on." In moments, the strains of *Gypsy Woman* fill the air. Mr. Fred does a Temptation two-step and turns.

"You don't know nothing about that kind of music do you, Miss Del?" he says, winking at me.

"Sure I do. Madame A has been playing those old records to me since I was a baby. You still got *Green Onions?*" I ask, looking at my grandmother.

"Yes indeed, unless somebody done come up in here while I was away and stole it."

"Play that one next," I request.

Mr. Fred shuffles through the LP's until he finds the correct one. "Come on, Doll, let's show this gal what real dancing is all about," he says, holding out his hand to Madame A. "That mess y'all doing now ain't no dancing. Y'all just rolling and grinding like you constipated. This here is the *real* deal."

Pulling Madame A close, they shuffle in time to the music before he swings her out, twirls her and pulls her close again. I hate to admit it, but Mr. Fred and Madame A have it going on. Caught up in the moment, I shimmy over to the stereo and load *Green Onions* to keep them going. As *Gypsy Woman* ends, I look over my shoulder and tell them, "Don't stop. Here comes *Green Onions*."

They pick up the pace and I watch in amazement as Madame A and Mr. Fred jerk in concert to the music. When Mr. Fred sidles up to Madame A's back and begins dancing butt-to-butt, rolling and grinding like they accused our generation of doing, I holler.

The song ends and they collapse on the couch, giggling and fanning at their faces. I place the cold glass of tea in Mr. Fred's hands and he promptly hands it to Madame A. "I'm gonna let her have this one. I'll just get another glass for myself," he says, lifting off the couch to walk towards the kitchen.

"I got it, Mr. Fred. Y'all looked good out there together. You know you kind of looked like me and my friends with you dancing behind her and all."

"What! Delphine Andrews I *know* you ain't out in public letting somebody dance on your behind!"

"No, Madame A. I meant the way he stood behind you and danced. The guys do that sometimes, but I don't let them get behind me. No sirree." I make a valiant attempt to keep a straight face, but fail when I hear Mr. Fred coughing and covering him mouth.

"Doll, now you danced like that when you was young and I know I did my share, so why wouldn't Miss Del be trying it out now? Like they say, 'ain't nothing new under the sun.' We did it in our time and now she's doing it in hers."

"Well, it don't seem *right* somebody dancing up behind my grandbaby like that."

"She your grandbaby, but she ain't no baby. Del, you what…18 or so?"

"Eighteen."

"Doll, didn't you get married when you was 16? Shoot, that gal actually running behind your schedule."

"You hush, you old devil you."

I return to the living room with the glass of iced tea. "Thank you. Hmmmm," he says, licking his lips.

"Your Moma makes some good tea. Tell her how much I appreciated it, will you?"

"Yes sir. You need anything else, Madame A?"

"No, baby. Me and Fred gonna sit here and talk awhile. You go on home."

Home? Did she forget I'm staying with her? "Ah....Madame A? I'm supposed to be staying here to help you around the house. Did you forget?"

Her jaw drops. "Goodness me, I sure did. Did you bring any clothes with you?"

"No ma'am."

"Why don't you go over and grab you a change of clothes. Fred will be here with me until you get back. How long you think it will take?"

"Maybe a half hour or so."

I see her wrinkle her nose. "Take your time. No rush. You just try to make it back before it gets dark. I know your mother will be worried sick if you're on the road and it's night."

"Okay." I retrieve my keys and quietly close the door as I walk to the car. *Why is she in a hurry to get me out of there?* Driving out, I look back through the window and their heads are already silhouetted as one. *That's why.*

Taking the turns in the road on the wrong side, I reach the house in a few minutes. I see Moma and Daddy walking out along the new rows of neatly turned earth. The bag she has in her hands and the hoe Daddy has in his tells me they are planting. They wave and I watch my mother walk hurriedly towards me, her face pinched into a frown as she reaches the fence.

"Del, what're you doing home?" she says out of breath.

"I just came to get some clothes."

"Why didn't you bring Mama with you? She could hurt herself alone at that house."

Uh oh. "She has…company… and she told me to come on and get my stuff."

"Who's over there? Maynard and Brenda?"

"No. Ah…Mr. Fred Chaps stopped by to see her."

"What! Fred has already done enough! They can't let her get home good before they back over there trying to help her break the other arm! Let me go in here and check on her." Moma turns to go towards the house.

"Moma!" I exclaim, grabbing her arm. "They're fine. Madame A is doing just fine."

"Hey, Del, everything all right?" my father asks, concern on his face as he looks from my mother to me.

"Yes, Daddy. I'm just here getting some clothes and—"

"Do you know that Fred Chaps is up at the house with Moma?" my mother interjects.

"And?" My father looks at her and says.

"She just got home *today* and he's already over there visiting with her."

"Well, Lee, she is a grown woman. I don't think Fred will do anything to her."

"That's not the point. She just got out and already her *men* are back in the picture like a pack of dogs. She needs her rest. She ain't got no time for no men to be visiting her."

"Shhhh. Calm down. Now Ms. Doll knows what she wants to do and Del's gonna go back over there when she gets her stuff together, so what's the big deal?"

"Moma could be *dead* by the time Del gets back over there! I knew I should have stayed over there, then this kind of mess wouldn't be going on."

"Del, how was Ms. Doll doing when you left?"

"She's was doing fine, Daddy. Her and Mr. Fred had danced to some records and they were—"

"Dancing! She needs to be sitting her butt down, not dancing! Fred needs to take his behind home. I'm going in here to check on her." She turns on her heels and walks with purpose towards the house.

"Lee? Your Moma is all right. Leave her alone," my Daddy calls after her. She shakes her head and flings her empty hand at him as she continues stomping towards the house. Looking back at me, he says, "I'm gonna stay out here. Ms. Doll's gonna tell her something she don't want to hear and I don't want to be nowhere close when she does. She needs to leave Ms. Doll alone and let live her own life. I could see if she was senile or something, but the only thing wrong with her Moma is she has man-itis. Get your stuff and go on back. I'm sure your Moma will be calling you tonight," he finishes, before turning and walking back to the garden.

I trudge to the house, knowing that if Moma starts in on Madame A, World War III will be initiated. Sure enough, the loud voice of my mother is heard as I walk into the living room.

"You need to be in the bed! That's the *main* reason why I let Del stay." She stops and listens.

"Fred needs to go home! I'm sending Del back over there just as soon as she gets her clothes together." I can tell she is exasperated by what she hears when she flings a fork into the sink.

"Moma, I want what's best for you and..." she stops and listens some more. "I am *not* trying to run your life! Don't forget, Fred helped you fall in the first place." She throws her hands in the air.

"Fine. I won't!" She finishes and chokes the phone before placing it back on the hook. Seeing me, she says, "Don't just stand there! Get your clothes together!"

I trot back to my bedroom and open my suitcase. Upsetting some books on my bed, the loud clatter wakes Weenie. He sticks his head out the door, sleep clinging to his eyes.

"What's all the noise about?" he asks slowly, rubbing at his sleepy eyes.

"It's Moma and Madame A. They're fighting on the phone."

"What they fighting about now?"

"Mr. Fred Chaps is over visiting Madame A and I came home to get some clothes and Moma is fit to be strangled."

I watch Weenie's eyes light up. "Mr. Fred is over there with Madame A right now?" I nod my head in the affirmative. "Hot dog! What they doing? They holding hands and kissing and stuff?"

"No. They were over there dancing before I left."

Walking into my room and closing the door, Weenie says, "See, *that's* what I'm talking about. Madame A got the men so flustered they can't *wait* to see her again. Old man Smithey ain't up there, is he?"

"No, just Mr. Fred."

"Now if ol' Smithey shows up, there might be fireworks for real. Can I go with you?"

"No, Weenie. You know you've got to stay here."

"Why? Me and Daddy finished the rows of the garden earlier today. I don't have to go to school, so I can visit with Madame A just like you."

"Madame A didn't suggest that you come and Moma is *not* in the mood for no requests like that one today. She is frothing at the mouth like she has rabies or something."

"I'll bet Moma's the one that called over there, didn't she?"

"You know she did. I don't know what Madame A told her, but she didn't take it too well."

"She knows she can't outtalk Madame A. She ought to just quit trying to mess in her *business*," Weenie says with plenty of attitude.

"Weenie, hush! Moma's gonna come down that hall and beat both of our butts if she hears you."

"Well, she should! Boy! I sure wish I could go on back over there with you 'cause I'll bet you my last week's *allowance* that Mr. Smithey gonna be over there before the night is through!" Weenie's eyes are shining now.

"I sure hope not! I don't know what I would do if both of them were over there at the same time."

"Ain't nothing for you to do. Just sit back and watch and make sure they don't get to pulling on

Madame A. Shoot! It's her world, not yours." He says this like he handles these type of situations everyday.

"Weenie, shut up and help me get these clothes in a bag. If I don't hurry up, Moma is gonna be up in here tripping for real."

"Moma's always tripping. If it's not Madame A, it's something else," he says absently.

"I know," I say, shaking my head, " but that's the way she is."

"This everything?" Weenie asks, looking at the clothes on the bed.

"That's all I need for a few days. I *can* come back and get something I forgot, you know."

"Hmmph. If Moma's acting like you say, she might not let you."

"Well, in that case, let's hope I got everything."

"I'll call you later on and see what's happening. Stay awake and try to remember everything," Weenie gives these last minute instructions.

"I *will*, Weenie."

"I'll walk you to the car. Moma might not act too bad if I'm with you."

"That hadn't stopped her before."

He thinks about this. "You right. Take your own bags."

"Weenie!"

"Bye, Del," he says quickly and runs to his bedroom, closing the door fast.

Gathering up my small suitcase, I trump down the hall and onto the front porch. My mother is sitting in one of the large rocking chairs, slowly moving herself backwards and forwards. She doesn't even glance up as I close the door.

"I'm gone, Moma." I say anxiously.

"Bye. I'll call and check on y'all later. If that other one shows up, you call me quick." I see daggers in her eyes as she says the last part.

"Okay, Moma." I put one foot on the stair tread.

"Del, you slow down on these roads. Remember that the cows get out around here. They can kill you if you hit them."

"I will. Bye." I trot down the steps.

"Bye."

Loading my things in the car, I wave to my father in the garden, slide in the car and begin backing out slowly. I keep the windows rolled tight, in case my mother has some last minute instructions. That way, I can tell her I didn't hear her.

Slowly, I navigate the road back to Madame A's, making sure I watch out for errant cows or prancing deer. Cresting the ridge, I breathe a sigh of relief when I spot only the truck in the drive. *At least Mr. Smithey didn't show up.*

The front door is locked as I try it. *What are they doing in there?* My minds runs through a few scenarios— some rather lusty—as I contemplate what to do next. Should I knock on the door or just sit out in the drive for a few minutes? My mother's pinched, accusing face flashes before my eyes and I find the courage to knock loudly. When there is no answer, I yell loudly, "Madame A! Madame A, are you all right? The door's locked!"

A hum I hadn't noticed before suddenly stops. Madame A's voice reaches me from behind the house, "Del? Del, we're on the patio. Come on back!"

The patio? Here I am scared they're getting their groove on or she's hurt or something, and they're out on the patio. I walk across the courtyard and around the brick fence. I watch where I place my feet when I near the chicken coop.

Rounding the side of the house, I stop, *amazed*, at the image before me. My grandmother and Mr. Fred are sitting in her hot tub, tall glasses of what I hope is iced tea placed on the sides. From the skinny straps and abundance of skin visible, Madame A either has on a bathing suit or is in her underwear. The bare, hairy chest of Mr. Fred stares boldly back at me.

Wonder what he has on under the water? I know he didn't just happen to bring over some bathing trunks.

Afraid of the answers, I stop the thoughts crowding my mind. Looking closely, I see that Madame A has wrapped her casted arm in a blue garbage bag and is holding it over the side, keeping it dry.

Seeing me, she calls out loudly, "Del, you got a swim suit?"

I stare at her, dumbstruck.

"You got one? Girl, what's *wrong* with you? If you've got one, put it on and get in the spa. This water is *right!*" Madame A urges me.

Mr. Fred, lounging next to her says, "Sho' is. You better hop on in here, girl."

"Ah...ah...I think I'll pass. I'll just go on in the house and watch some TV." The *last* thing I want to do is get in a hot tub with my grandmother and her boyfriend. Talk about uncomfortable.

"You sure? We don't mind you joining us, now," Madame A giggles, her eyes flashing happily.

"That's okay. I'll be fine in the house."

"All right then. Hey Del...grab that radio over by the counter and bring it out here."

Finding the radio where she indicated it was, I bring it out to the patio.

"Now, turn it to WTIJ. They play blues and oldies in the evenings." Turning the knob, I locate the station. "That's it. Thank you, baby."

Walking back inside, I say, "Call me if y'all need anything."

"We'll be fine. You just watch your TV and go to bed when you feel like it. Oh, and no phone calls for me. Tell them I'm *indisposed* tonight," Madame A giggles. She then flips a switch and the spa begins humming again.

I watch television, interspersed with tiptoeing to the curtain to look at the two aging lovebirds in the hot tub and answering the phone, until it watches me. Awaking some time later, the house is quiet. Looking at the clock, I realize that it is after midnight. *Why didn't somebody wake me up?* A glance in the backyard reveals no one. Peering down the hallway, I see a light is still on in Madame A's room. I walk down the hallway and knock lightly.

"Yes?" Madame A's slow voice reaches me.

"I was just checking on you."

"I'm fine. I'm already in the bed."

"You need anything?"

"Nothing. Go on to bed. Use the front bedroom, near the kitchen. It's the largest and the nicest."

That's strange. Usually, I sleep in the one next to hers. "Okay, then. See you in the morning."

"G'night, baby."

"'Night."

I sleepily wash my face and brush my teeth before sinking into the soft bed. Dreams begin to assault me as I pull the covers over my body.

CHAPTER

7

I awake the next morning to the sound of a car cranking up. I can tell by the faint sunlight it's early morning so I'm surprised to hear a car. I struggle to sit up to find out who is visiting this time of the day, but I catch only the red glow of the taillights in the distance as the vehicle crests the hill. Entering the kitchen, I see my grandmother sitting at the table, a cup of hot tea resting in front of her. An empty cup sits in front of the chair next to her.

"Hey. What'cha you doing up so early?" I ask, rubbing sleep from my eyes. Glancing at the clock, I see that it is only 6:30.

"It's not early for the country. I've been up a little while."

"Oh, I forgot. I was planning to fix you a big breakfast and bring it to you."

"You still can."

"Who was just here?"

"Oh, nobody."

"You didn't hear the car leaving the drive?" I stare at her, confused. She couldn't have missed the car if she was sitting right there facing the front door.

"I heard it," she says succinctly and resumes sipping from her cup.

"O...kay." *What's up with that?* Guess I don't need to know. "Let me wash my face and I'll get on the breakfast."

"Take your time, baby, I'm not going anywhere anytime soon."

Entering the bathroom, I quickly wash my hands and face. Brushing my teeth, I falter when I see the men's shorts hung over the shower rod in the bathroom. *Who's shorts are those?* Suddenly it dawns on me—they are Mr. Fred's shorts. *Guess I know what he had on in the spa.* I shudder.

Leaving the bathroom, I tell Madame A, "Ah...Mr. Fred must have left his shorts. There are some hanging up in the bathroom."

"Did he? He'll remember sometime or the other and be back," Madame A says nonplused.

"So what time did he leave?" I ask curiously. I never heard him leave last night, so I guess it was while I was asleep on the couch.

"Oh, I don't know. It was early though." A smile tugs at the corners of her mouth.

"He seems like a nice man," I say.

"He is. Fred makes me feel like I'm twenty again. Can't tell it by looking at him, but that devil has a wild streak painted *straight* down his back."

Mr. Fred *wild*? Well, I didn't expect to find him in the hot tub, so maybe he is just a little…wild.

"Uh hum. That Fred makes me *happy*."

"That's good." I'm glad she's in such a good mood this morning. "You want some bacon with eggs and grits?"

"That's fine. Whatever you cook, I'll eat."

"How long have you been seeing Mr. Fred?"

"I've known Fred since he was a little child. We didn't start seeing each other until a few months ago, though."

"He sure seems to like you a lot."

"Oh, he does. He *surely* does."

The way she said it makes me take notice of her. Madame A has on a silk Oriental robe, with slits running high up the sides. Looking down, I realize that I can see her plump legs all the way to the top of her thighs. No gown is peeking through the slit at all! *Is she naked under that robe?* Glancing upwards, I can see her breasts moving unfettered beneath the robe as she lifts her arm for her cup. *Oh my goodness! What in the world?* My eyes grow round as saucers as I realize that she is indeed naked.

"You can just quit looking like that. Yes, that was Fred just leaving this morning and yes, he spent the night."

Hot dang a doo! Madame A's still knocking boots at her age. "Wha...wha...ah.."

"Close your mouth, girl, you 'bout to catch a stray fly."

I snap my mouth closed.

"Ain't nothing wrong with spending time with somebody you care for."

"But...but..." I stutter, still in disbelief at what I just heard.

"Nothing. I'm old enough and I got a consenting partner, so nothing."

"Okay," I finally manage to say. I turn to the stove to contemplate all this overinformation a little more. Seventy-five years old and still having sex! I thought folks quit that when they got fifty or so. Guess not. I sure hope she's practicing safe sex. Oh my goodness, do they even *sell* "protection" to folks that old?

"Madame A, can I ask you something?" I ask with trepidation.

"Sure, baby, what is it?"

"Since I know you like Mr. Fred and all...what about your other boyfriend?"

"Smithey? What about him?"

"You're not seeing him in the same...*way*, are you?"

Holding her hands in the air, she looks towards the heavens and says, "Lord, I *knew* the day would come when my granddaughter would be talking under my skirt, but give me the *strength* to not cuss her behind out." She finally lowers her hands and looks at me. "Now, I don't *normally* go 'round discussing my business in the streets. Don't nobody need to know what's going on but me and the person I got the going ons with. *But*, since you are probably shocked about me and Fred, I'm gonna answer you. Yes, I am seeing Smithey the same way I'm seeing Fred. Satisfied?"

Oooh wee! Wait until I tell Weenie about this! "Ah...you like Mr. Smithey like you like Mr. Fred?"

"No. I like them in two, totally different ways."

How many different ways can you like a man? Either you like him or not, right? "But...you're sleeping with *both* of them."

"Yes, and I've got a few more on my list to get through before y'all shovel the dirt on my coffin."

List? Madame A's got a man list?!

"Madame A," I start slowly and calmly, "you've got to be careful nowadays. There's so much out there you can catch." *I read the pamphlets!*

"Oh, don't you worry about me none. I've been practicing safe sex since before they came out with it. I *always* get them to 'wrap it up'. If they don't want to wrap it, then they can keep on trucking. Ain't nobody gonna give me *shit*! After I had had my kids and they came out with the pill, I was one of the first ones in line. Then later, when that wasn't an issue anymore, I switched to good old rubbers. Girl, them female rubbers are something else! Ain't no reason to get a baby or nothing else from a joker but the good time you trying to get these days."

This is *definitely* way too much information for me.

"You get them fellas to use protection when you doing it, too. I ain't worried about AIDS and stuff at my age, but I'm worried about you. I don't want you to catch something and die before me."

"Oh, grandmother!"

"It's true. Just the other day, I read in the paper how some fella was running around having sex with everybody and he knew he was infected with AIDS. He managed to get a few other girls infected before they caught him. If I was their folks, I would save the county a bunch of money. I'd pop a cap in his ass *quick* as I could find him."

I begin laughing, thinking how she probably *would* shoot somebody.

"That mess ain't right. If you got it, deal with it. Let somebody else *chose* whether or not they like you enough to die for you. Hmmph."

"Well, when I finally *start* having sex, I will be careful."

"Please."

"Now, what else you want for breakfast?" I ask, finished with this conversation for now.

"Grab some of those muscadine preserves your Moma sent over and that should do it."

It surely will.

CHAPTER

The morning plods along slowly as we watch soap operas and game shows nonstop. My mother calls, of course, and manages to put a damper on things with her comments. I can tell by the look in Madame A's eyes, she is glad my mother is *not* here. I take a TV break, with relief, during "The Young and Restless" to begin cooking lunch.

Just as I get the chicken breasts in the skillet, I hear a car driving up to the door. Opening the door, I see my Aunt Brenda stepping out of an older model Cadillac, one of those long ones that you see pimps sporting in movies and stuff, but are still common modes of transportation around here. Her two daughters and some smaller children get slowly out behind her. Seeing me, she waves as she helps a small girl to the ground.

"Hey, Del," she says, hugging me briefly.

"How you doing, Aunt Brenda?" I ask.

"I've definitely had better times," she replies in a tired voice. Up close, I can tell that plenty has been on her mind since I last saw her. The crow's feet crowd around her sunken, dark eyes; her hair looks dry and barely combed; and her clothes are wrinkled all over. She looks older that Madame A. "Where is Mama?"

"She's in the living room watching her stories." Turning to my cousins, Carla and Laquinsa, I see they are done up in what country folks think is ghetto-fabulous style, as always. The tall, baked on hairdo with blue yarn woven through it that Carla is sporting, makes her head appear larger than her body. Laquinsa's hair, on the other hand, has grown at least two feet since Christmas.

"Hey Carla, Laquinsa, how's it going?" I say. Sullenly, they reply something unintelligible to my ears. That's nothing new. They always picked on me and Weenie and still try. "Who are these little kids?" I ask.

"School made you crazy, Del? Them my kids Herman, Dominisha, and Tralph." Carla manages to say with disgust on her face.

"Oh. I haven't seen them in a while. Well, come on in."

In the background I can hear Carla saying low to Laquinsa, "Who she thinks she is telling us to come in? She's our grandmother just like she's hers. This ain't her house anyway. Why she up in here?" I ignore the snotty voice and continue walking into the house.

Madame A is so engrossed in the story line, she doesn't even lift her head when we enter. Calling out brightly, I say, "Madame A, look who's here!"

Turning her head briefly, she sees the visitors and motions for them to sit down before returning to her soap opera. The children begin asking for soda and crackers and to use the bathroom. Their mother apparently has gone deaf since she just plops on a couch and begins watching television.

"Y'all know where the bathroom is. Leave Del alone," my aunt finally tells them. "Ain't nobody getting *nothing* to eat 'cause you should have eaten before we left. I told y'all that."

The soap opera finally ends. Madame A is all smiles as she turns to the people gathered on the furniture. "Did you see that Victor Newman? And Nicky ought to sit her old behind down. How many times she gonna try to remarry that man? If it didn't work the first three times, it ain't gonna work the fourth time either." Madame A shakes her head disgusted. "So, Brenda, I see you finally found your way over here. What you need now?"

"Mama, why you always acting like the only time I come over here is when I need something?"

"'Cause you usually *do* need something when you come over. What is it this time?"

"I came over here to check up on you. I couldn't get to the hospital...my car was in the shop and I was wondering how you were, that's all."

"I'm fine. Now what do you need?" Madame A asks again.

Aunt Brenda sighs and looks at the floor. "Well...I...*could* use a few dollars...just until I get my check next month and all. I need a little food...and anyway, I'll pay you right back."

"Brenda, I've told you time and time again, you get enough to live on. You need to manage your money better. What's the problem?" Looking over at my cousins, she says, "Carla and Laquinsa, y'all ain't back over to your Mama's house, now are you?"

They look at her boldly, but don't reply.

"Brenda, I told you to keep them girls out your house. They too old to be freeloading off of you."

"We don't freeload off of *nobody*," Carla barks. "She watches my kids and I give her food stamps and stuff."

"What about some money? They ain't taking food stamps for rent now, are they?" My aunt shakes her head. "That's what I thought. Y'all should be ashamed that you got your big asses up in that house with her and she's over here trying to borrow some money. Where's y'all's money?"

"Moma, this is only a temporary thing. They're gonna move out just as soon as they get back on their feet," Aunt Brenda says quickly, trying to calm Madame A.

"You mean get up off their *butts*," Madame A states harshly.

Aunt Brenda begins to protest, "Mama, they—"

Madame A stops her with, "Hush, Brenda, I've held my tongue long enough." Looking at my cousins, she says, "Now, your mama may not have been the *best* mother in the world, but she tried pretty hard. With your daddy coming and going like he wanted and working and bringing home money when he felt like it, things were not normal, like a lot of other children. *But*, she still kept y'all together, fed and clean. Seems like the *least* you could do is help her out around *her* house. She's been sick and I can tell ain't nobody been taking care of her like they should. She don't need all these kids running in and out, sick as she's been. Now, if you wanted a houseful of kids, then I'm assuming that you were ready to keep a houseful of kids and everything that goes with them. Carla, ain't you getting child support and welfare?"

Carla nods her head briefly.

"That's what I thought. Laquinsa, you still work at Wal-Mart?"

Laquinsa shakes her head in the negative.

"What happened this time?" Madame A says, disgust in her voice.

"The manager was always picking on me," Laquinsa pouts.

"Picking on you. How?"

"He was always saying that the customers complained about me talking to the other cashiers while I was scanning their stuff."

"Were you?"

"Not really. Sometimes one of the other cashiers would come up and tell a joke and I would laugh and make some comments, but it wasn't all the time."

"So he fired you?"

"No. I got sick and tired of him coming over every night with another complaint, so I told him he could have his funky job. I *quit,*" Laquinsa states indignantly.

"Where're you working now?"

Laquinsa looks down at the floor. "Nowhere."

"You quit without having another job to go to and now, you ain't got no job at all. I know you ain't getting unemployment 'cause you quit on your own." Madame A stares at Laquinsa hard. "This is a fine, damn mess. Y'all make the jacked up choices and Brenda has to bail you out *and* support you too. Now, y'all done drained her and you had *her* come over here to get some money to support both of y'all's big behinds, plus kids. Look at you! Hair and nails *hooked up*! And you ain't got no money for food. Ain't something wrong with this picture to you?" She looks from Aunt Brenda to Carla to Laquinsa. They avoid her eyes.

"I'm telling you girls now, if something happens to your mother, you gonna be in a *world* of shit. I ain't *about* to support no healthy adults and I know Lena and Maynard ain't gonna either. You ain't seen your daddy since Jesse Jackson ran for president. Who you gonna be depending on? Yourself or some man in the street, that's who. Now, I'm gonna give you a little money, Brenda, but I'm also gonna have them deliver some groceries to you. That way, at least I know you and the kids will be eating."

Rushing over to hug her, my aunt says, "Thank you Mama. I'm gonna pay you back just as soon as I get my check."

"I know you will, baby, but you ain't the one need to be thanking me." She eyes the girls hard. "You get yourself some rest. I'll be over to check up on you in the next few days."

With tears threatening to fall, Aunt Brenda, hugs Madame A tightly. "Thank you so much. You just don't know how much I needed this little help. Thank you, Mama, thank you."

"You're welcome baby. Now get on out of here and lie down. I'm gonna call over to Hollister's Grocery in just a few minutes. One of y'all *can* answer the door and put up the groceries, can't you?" Madame A asks pointedly at Laquinsa and Carla.

"Yes ma'am," they chorus.

Leaving much faster than they entered, they pile into the car. Madame A writes a check and the dust flows from their tracks in moments.

"Hmmph. Them girls gonna be the death of Brenda. Healthy, grown ass women still living with their Mama. Damn shameful. Del, you stay up in school and finish so you can get you a good job. Don't be no burden on your folks. When you get old and have raised your kids, you ain't looking for no more. Remember that."

"I will."

"Well, I'm hungry. What'd you cook?"

"I fried the chicken breasts Moma left out and I got some macaroni with cheese cooking now."

"That sounds good. How long until we eat?"

"Maybe fifteen minutes of so."

"Well, I guess I'll just grab a glass of tea and keep you company until then," she says settling into a kitchen chair. "You all right about this morning?"

"I'm fine. I was just...surprised and all."

"Ain't no need to be surprised. Anything dead needs to be buried and ain't *nothing* dead on me!" she says with a laugh.

"I can see that. Ah, Madame A, you seem to like all types of men. I saw some of the photos where...where there was a white man in them that wasn't Grandpa Bernie. Who was that?"

"What did he look like?"

How many white men has she dated? "Well, he was tall, with light-colored hair."

"Good looking?"

"Yes."

"Well, that was either Smithey when he was younger or Thumper."

"Thumper?" That *definitely* was a white person's name. They're always naming their kids Tab or Biff or something else totally out there.

"Yeah, Thumper Douglas. You know Douglas Lumber Company over in Natchez?"

"Oh, yeah."

"He's the daddy of the Douglas boy running the place now."

"And y'all dated?" *Madame A sure was busy, especially with the climate of that time.*

"Sure did. On the sly, of course. Me and Thumper was in *love*."

102

"What did the folks have to say?"

"Well, it never got to be public knowledge. Wouldn't nobody have found out at all, except this was back during the late fifties or early sixties and me and him couldn't get no hotel room. They didn't let the colored folks stay in *their* hotels back then. So, me and Thumper had to meet in the woods back behind my folks' house."

"The woods?"

"Yes. Girl, you ain't *had none* until you had it out in the open woods." She says this like it was the Second Coming of you know who. "Anyway, one day we were over there and my Daddy comes up and catches us hugging and stuff. My clothes were wrapped around me any which-a-way and Thumper had his shirt off, so my daddy knew what was going on right off."

"How embarrassing!" I would just *die* if my folks caught me making out with a boy.

"Shoot, I didn't have time for embarrassment. My daddy picked up a stick and started hitting me all over my back and arms. Thumper got so scared, he just hopped in his pickup truck and left."

"He didn't try to stop your daddy?"

"No. My daddy was a big man—six four, black and muscular. Wasn't no man about to tussle with him unless he had a gun and some backup."

103

"What happened next?"

"My daddy beat me, a grown woman with three kids, all the way back up to the house. He told my mama what happened and she started crying and screaming that I was a tramp and that the Klu Klux Klan was gonna come and kill us all. See, my mama was a bible-carrying, professed, Christian woman, but she was mean as a snake. She had thirteen kids and she was real protective of us all. She made sure we stayed close to home and avoided white folks as much as we could Wasn't no way that we could just run around doing anything and everything. When Daddy said that stuff about Thumper and me, she was fit to be tied."

"Dog! What did you do then?"

"My mother and father got my cousin, Lester, to come and take me to my grandmother over in Magee— Big Moma. Now, Big Moma was a full-blooded Natchez Indian and she walked with a cane. I didn't want to go 'cause Big Moma was meaner than Mama. When we were little she would call us names and cuss us out, so I wasn't too particular about her. After Lester dropped me off and told her what had happened, I could see by her pinched face, I was gonna have a miserable time there. Sure enough, she tried to act like I was a slave or something. She'd grab me and the kids with her cane when she wanted something and we weren't fast enough for her. I even saw her hitting my Uncle Cleophus with that cane, and he was about fifty then. Just mean, straight to the core."

"Were there any problem for your parents?" I ask.

"Naw. No Nightriders came or anything, so after a few weeks, I came on back home."

"You ever talk to the man again?"

"I saw him about twenty years later, but he acted like he didn't know me, so I acted the same."

They're still doing it, too. Boys always act like they don't know you when situations go bad. All tongue-tied and scared when their "friend" shows up. Like they don't know how they got down to the mall holding your hand. *Please!*

"That must have hurt."

"No. It's the way things are. One thing I learned from all that is, no matter what, they're always gonna blame the woman. The man can get away with *murder*, they still gonna pin the whole mess on the woman's head. You got to learn to get it while the gettings good, 'cause when it's over for them, it's over for you."

"That not fair, blaming the woman for everything," I say, indignant.

"Del, fare is what you pay for a taxi ride, train ride and a bus seat. Ain't nothing else fair in life."

"I'll remember that, Madame A."

"Make sure that you do. Let's eat."

We bow our heads to say grace. The ringing of the phone starts just as we finish our blessing.

"Who in the world is calling while we're trying to eat?" Madame A says absently. "If it's one of them telemarketer people, get their name and tell them I'll call them right back just as *soon* as I finish up with my plate of food," she says, as she lifts the food to her mouth. "I don't know what's wrong with people nowadays. They act like they don't know what time lunch is. Don't they eat lunch? Just makes me plumb sick—"

"Hello?" I say into the phone, cutting off Madame A.

"Miss Del?" a man asks.

"Yes?" *I wonder who this is?*

"How ya doing? This is Fred Chaps. Sho' is a fine day today, isn't it?"

"Yessir, it sure is," I say as my eyes are involuntarily drawn to the windows to stare out at the beautiful day.

"Sure wish I was somewhere else but up in here," Mr. Fred continues with a sigh. "Guess I'm just feeling a touch of that 'Spring Fever.'"

"You're not the only one, Mr. Fred." I see Madame A motioning for the phone, but I hold my hand up so that he can finish. It's very rude to just hand a phone over to someone else while the person is still talking. Madame A taught me that. She gives me a mild evil-eye look, but I still hold the phone while he talks on.

"Yeah, I can see the kids taking to the yard and some of them girls that came into the store today...Lawdamercy! Let the temperature get a little above 60 degrees and they forget their clothes. Some of them looked like they're ready to try out for a pole spot up at the Pudding Palace," he finishes with a chuckle. The Pudding Palace is a strip joint that just opened in Natchez. Sounds like he might have already been up in there since he knows about the poles. "Next week, their momas are gonna be up in here trying to get something for the flu they asking for walking around here half-naked. Old Man Winter ain't got his claws out of Lady Spring just yet!"

"You're probably right," I respond while Madame A motions for the phone again. *Hold on*, I mouth to her.

"Yes indeed. In fact, I need to call and stock up on some cough syrup and cold medicine 'cause I imagine it's gonna be a run on them items next week. Yessiree. We gonna be busy next week. I can tell." He continues on. "Miss Del, would Miss Doll happen to be up and around?"

"Yessir, she is. Let me hand her the phone." I place the phone in Madame A's waiting hands.

" 'Bout time. You act like he was calling here for you or something," she says, acting offended, but I know she really isn't.

"Hello Fred." She purrs into the phone. "I was just thinking about you..."

"Tonight? Oh, I'm sorry, but me and Del have already planned something for tonight," she says, as I stare at her incredulously.

What do we already have planned? I mouth to her.

She dismisses my question with a wave of her hand and keeps on talking. "Tomorrow? Well...I don't know..." she stops and listens. "How late you talking?"

She huffs before she answers. "I don't know about after nine. You know I *need* my beauty rest. I can't just be up late too many nights." She listens again. "That was *so* sweet. You need to quit filling my head up with mess like that."

"Ah hmmmm." Her voice drops and she turns to face the opposite wall. "Is that right?"

"Well, you forgot your shorts and about scared Del to death..."

"She's alright now, though..."

"Nine o'clock is still too late. You got to get over here earlier if you want us to be able to spend any *quality* time together..."

"I know things are busy, but you got to make time for me. I'm not gonna be just slid into any ol' available spot. I got to get a *quality* time slot..."

"I tell you what. You give me a call early in the day and we'll just go from there..."

"You take care too. I'll talk to you tomorrow?"

"Bye now." Madame A finishes with a slick, cat grin on her face. "What?" she asks me.

"Where, exactly, are we going tonight?"

"I don't know, but you got to keep them guessing. You can't make yourself too available 'cause then they think that my world revolves only around them and they try to treat me any old kind of way. That's right, keep them guessing and things stay *fresh* a lot longer," she says, clucking her tongue.

"You don't let your boyfriends visit after nine o'clock?" Stefan doesn't get to the dorm to visit me until after nine most nights. We don't even go out on dates until *after* ten o'clock sometimes!

"No indeed not! I will *not* be treated as an afterthought. You're gonna have to act like you *want* to spend time with me. You ain't gonna just show up here like I'm the 'after dark' entertainment." She shakes her head for emphasis.

"I know what you mean. Sometimes the boys at college want to come and visit you only at night. When they see you around campus, they act like they barely know you and then later, they're begging you to come down and talk to them. It's confusing. You never know where you really stand with them," I say, thinking about the up and down rollercoaster relationship I have with Stefan. One day, he acts like he doesn't have time for me, then the next, he's all over me.

"Well, missy, you need to stop that kind of mess before it even gets started. Make those jokers *work* to see you. Don't be giving in to any old kind of foolishness. If they only want to see you in the dark and can't speak to you in the light, why that just down right disrespectful. They acting like you a 'lady of the evening' or something. They ain't trying to treat you like you're supposed to be treated. You're way better than that mess."

"Yeah." I say with conviction I don't feel.

"I tell you, and I don't know *why* I'm telling you all about my life now, but anyway, one time, I had a fella that I thought was all hotstuff. Girl, that man was cocoa-brown and made me tongue-tied whenever I ran into him," she says with a dreamy look on her face.

Dog, that man must have been something to make Madame A tongue-tied!

"Raymond Miller was his name. That man was something to look at. Mmm*mmm*! Things started out real good—now this was after I came back from Chicago with the kids the last time. He would take me and the kids to the fair and shopping over in Natchez sometimes and he *loved* to take me out on long Sunday drives. Girl, I could barely wait for church to be over so I could ride the road with him," she says, fanning at her flushed face.

The way she's acting, those Sunday drives must have included some "off-road" driving.

"But after a few months, he started missing our drives and all but stopped taking me and the kids anyplace. He just wanted to come over for a few minutes on his way home from work, most times, and he didn't even get off work until 6:30. By the time he drove here from Brookhaven and got a shower, it was after 8 o'clock—just when I needed to be getting the kids to bed or helping with homework or getting myself ready for the next day. When my folks started commenting on the time he was stopping by, I talked to him about it. He just stopped by, all dirty and stuff from the mill, and sit and talked a few minutes before he left. I tried to work with him. I figured he was working hard and was probably too tired to take me and the kids all around like he used to."

"But one day, Del, and it hurts me to tell this to *anybody*," Madame A says, clutching her chest, her eyes sad, "one day, I decided to take the kids to Natchez and do some shopping. We had just come out of Krafts Five and Dime down there on Main Street, where that big bank is now? I was loading our stuff in the truck and lo' and behold, who do I see strutting down the street, all dressed up and with a woman hanging onto his arm? Raymond. He looked up, saw me then *crossed...over* to the other side of the street. Didn't say a word! Didn't acknowledge me or anything! Just acted like I wasn't even there! Del, I got so mad, I wanted to *cuss* that S.O.B. out right there on the street! I had *lowered* my standards by letting that *chump* come and visit me any old hour, thinking he didn't have time to take me places and do things like we use to, and here he is out on the town, in broad damn daylight, with some other woman. I felt lower than the *dirt* I was standing on! Just terrible. He only acted like that 'cause he thought I was desperate and what's so bad is, I let him! *That's* why you've got to have high standards and make them live up to your standards. Don't just take whatever comes your way just 'cause he's a man. Make him *work* to spend up some of your good time," she finishes harshly.

"Yes ma'am, I will." And I meant it to. Slowly, but surely, I was starting to rethink how I had been allowing boys to treat me.

"Let's finish eating 'cause I feel a nap coming on," she says, shaking her head. "Wooowee. I didn't mess up your digestion, did I?" She looks at me apologetically.

"No ma'am. I love hearing you talk about your life."

"Don't just *listen*, take some of it to heart, girl."

"Yes ma'am."

"Eat up 'cause the couch is calling my name."

CHAPTER

9

Evening finds me lethargic and sluggish from the naps I managed off and on during the afternoon. Madame A snores loudly across the room, mouth gaped open; her tongue occasionally licking her full lips. I stare at this fountain of knowledge as she sleeps—seventy-five years old, a world traveler, a great-grandmother, and she still manages to find time to date regularly. Shoot! I want to be just like her when I grow up.

BRRIINNGGGG!

The ringing phone pulls my attention from her. Madame A jolts awake and I rush to quickly answer it. It's probably Moma or Weenie calling to check up on us again.

"Hello."

Humming greets my ears.

"Hello?"

"Ah...is Fred Chaps there?" a woman's voice asks me.

"No ma'am, he isn't," I reply, wondering if something had changed and Mr. Fred was planning to visit anyway.

"Is he expected anytime soon?" the woman huffs.

"I don't...know. Hold on, let me let you speak to my grandmother." I walk across the room and hand the phone to Madame A, who mouths, *Who is it?* With a shrug of my shoulders, I hand her the phone and walk back to reclaim my spot on the couch.

"Yes?" Madame A says into the phone.

"Who is this?" she listens briefly.

"Bertha, Fred don't live here. You tried his store?" Harsh now.

"Well, I don't know where he is—"

"That's something you need to be asking Fred, not me—" I could tell Madame A was getting pissed at being cut off and she showed how pissed she was in another second.

"Now, you wait *one minute*, young lady. You don't call over to my house with this *mess*. If you and Fred got a problem, then *y'all* fix it. Don't get me in the middle of y'all's mess—"

"I've heard all I want to hear, now don't call over here again unless you and I got some *real* business. Good day." With that she motions for me to get the phone and hang it up.

"Who was that?" I ask, intrigued by the one-sided conversation I heard.

"Bertha Harris."

"Is that one of Mr. Fred's kids?"

"No. She was his common-law wife. He moved out a year or so back and she tries to run off any woman she *thinks* is interested in him. She knows better than to call over here looking for him. I told her about that mess a few weeks back."

"You don't think she's coming over here, do you?" I ask with fear rising around my heart as I contemplate the possibly ugly scene.

"Naw. Bertha got way more sense than that. If she does, she sho' gonna wish she hadn't." Madame A says with pursed lips, eyes rolling.

"You sure?" I say, not feeling reassured about the situation.

"Positive. Rest your nerves, girl. Ain't nobody coming out here to whip up on your old grandmama no time soon."

"What if they're still seeing each other? Mr. Fred might not be telling the whole truth about the situation." *Boys do that all the time.*

"I don't care if they're wrapped up in a lip-lock every night. That's something Fred got to deal with, not me. Fred is a grown man and he ain't married to me or nobody else. The only way I plan to stop seeing him is if he doesn't want to see me."

"But I just don't want you to get hurt or nothing. Women act a *fool* about men these days."

"Baby, they've *been* acting a fool about men for thousands of years. This situation ain't no different from millions of others. The thing I don't understand about these women though, if you're trying to keep your man in line, why are you going through the supposed 'girlfriend?' Why not work it through the man? The way they go about it, they working with the tail and not the head and last time I looked, the tail of nothing never controlled the head."

"I see what you mean."

"See that you do. Oh, Smithey Zacharias didn't call while I was napping, did he?"

"No ma'am. The only calls we got was Moma, Mr. Fred earlier and that one."

"Did your mama say she was coming over?"

"She didn't say for sure, but you know how she is. She might pop over here any minute to make sure that Mr. Fred doesn't show back up."

"She's subject to do that too." Yawning widely, she says, "I don't know about you, but I don't want to do anything tonight."

"Don't."

"I wish I could, but tonight, I've got choir practice. I missed the past two weeks laid up in the hospital, so I need to try and make it tonight."

"If you're tired, just rest. They've been getting along fine without you these few weeks, another one won't make a difference."

"Baby, I've got an obligation to go. There ain't but a few of us left as it is and when one of us is out, you can tell."

"What time does it start?"

"Six-thirty. We'll just grab a little dinner and go on over there."

"All right."

I rise and began making some chicken salad with the leftover breasts from lunch. Madame A goes to her room to freshen up and change. Eating quickly, I pile the dishes in the sink for later and we head over to the church.

δ

Mercy Saddle Missionary Church.

People are always asking me how the church got its name. The story I heard was that some nuns first built the church and named it Mercy Saddle. After they died out, the people in the community bought the land and added the Missionary Church to it. With its gothic lines and stained glass windows, it is an unusual site, to say the least, in these parts.

Reverend Ezekiel Blackjack has been pastor since I was a child. Reverend Blackjack has got plenty of problems—adultery, outside children, embezzlement of church funds—but the people overlook them all and flock to hear his deep, melodious voice every Sunday. A few months ago, somebody shot up his house. Now he's walking around with an "entourage" of four bodyguards. What kind of Lord's work gets you shot at in Yokel? I pointed this out the last time I was home and Moma told me to stay out of other folk's business. Looks like I ain't the only one need to stay out of other folk's business. Oh well.

Pulling into the gravel parking lot, I see a smattering of cars already parked near the entrance.

"Pull over there next to the Buick. I don't want to walk too far when we get finished," Madame A tells me.

Miss June Lett, gray-haired, humped-back woman and one of Madame A's oldest friends, opens the door and gingerly descends the stairs, her hands choking the life out of the guardrail. I watch her closely as I help Madame A out of the car.

"June! They 'bought to get started?" Madame A calls out to her.

"Yeah. The musician is warming up the piano right now. How you doing, Doll?"

"Just fine. I've been taking it easy, getting plenty of rest."

"That's good. Lena coming tonight?"

"She didn't say, but I imagine she is."

"I forgot my glasses so I'll see y'all in a minute."

Taking our time, I slowly help Madame A up the steep steps of the church. The sound of a piano played with beautiful precision floats to our ears. The last time I was at church, Miss Dump, an octogenarian fixture at the piano, was still trying to murder a hymn. She played the piano like it had done something to her. It's *definitely* not her playing right now.

"Who's playing for y'all now?" I ask.

"That's a new fella we got from Fayette."

"He sounds good."

"Chile, sometimes when I sit there and just listen to him, I think I'm already knocking at the Pearly Gates."

Opening the door, I walk behind her as she strolls down the center aisle. People are already gathered in the choir stand. Making introductions, I greet everyone and sit on the front pew. Peeking his head around the corner of the upright piano, the musician speaks briefly.

As he stands to get everyone's attention, I see that he is a young, slight man prone to dramatic gestures and, as he speaks, a high, strangled voice. After giving brief instructions, with a flourish of his manicured hands, he begins playing a new, contemporary Gospel song. The choir members stumble along, trying to get acquainted with the words and the beat of the music. Madame A's deep contralto booms loudly as they reach the chorus. He stops suddenly and looks at her.

"Ms. Doll, we know you got a good voice, but don't forget you got other folks to help you out with the song. This *ain't* no solo," he says in his falsetto voice.

"I know that."

"Let's try it again from the chorus."

He begins playing and this time Madame A lowers the volume of her voice. As they near the end, the members seem to become confused and everyone is singing different words. The piano keeps on to the end.

"That was good for a first try. Let's do it again." The musician smiles.

"What do you mean 'that was good?' We're all singing different words at the end. That ain't right. You need to clear this up for us," Madame A snaps, confusion on her face.

"You singing different words 'cause you're supposed to. The altos got their part; the sopranos theirs;

and the tenors and basses, a different one. It's a three-part harmony."

"You mean we're *supposed* to sound like this?" Disbelief mars her features.

"Yes. Haven't you heard this song on the radio?"

"I can't say that I have. It must sound a whole lot better that we do 'cause I don't recognize it," Madame A huffs.

"The more we practice it, the better it will sound," he assures her.

"If you say so," Madame A responds with a shrug of her shoulders.

"Let's try it again from the top." The musician starts his intro and the choir members segue in with gusto.

The door opens and my mother hurries down the aisle, Weenie dragging behind her. Patting my arm, she walks into the choir stand and takes her place. Weenie plops down besides me, a sullen look on his face.

"Hey, what's up?"

"Nothing. Moma knows I didn't want to come out here with her," Weenie pouts.

"You weren't doing anything at home, so what's wrong with coming with her? She probably wanted you to drive." I bump his arm playfully.

"Naw. She's always dragging me down here. She hopes I'll join the Junior choir or something."

"That new musician y'all got sure will make you sing." My head was bopping to the beat of his music.

"Not me. I don't want to be up in no choir lead by Sweets," Weenie says, his eyebrow lifted high.

"That's his *name*?" I ask, wondering what kind of mother named her child Sweets.

"That's what I call him 'cause if you look close, you'll see he has cake in both of his back pockets," Weenie clarifies.

"Quit!"

"He does. Look at him! You ever seen a man with fingernails that long? And he wears clear fingernail polish on them, too."

"Maybe he just likes to keep his hands nice."

"All them kind of men like to keep their hands *nice*. Just like *girls* do."

"Now, Weenie, Moma told you about judging folks."

"I ain't judging him, I'm telling the truth. Anyway, he goes with Reverend Blackjack's grandson."

"Stop *lying*! You up in *church*!" I whisper fiercely. Lying in church is *way worse* than just lying every place else. It's blasphemy.

"I'm *not* lying! You go to town sometimes. They ride around in this Miata convertible, sitting close and everything. Daddy makes me look away when they ride through."

"I guess he thinks there are some things you just don't need to see."

"I'm sixteen, not six. We've got a couple of those 'fun boys' up at school."

My mother takes this opportunity to shush us and we fall silent. Our silence lasts only a minute before Weenie asks me to step outside with him. Tiptoeing quietly, we walk outside and sit on the steps.

"Del, what happened the other night? You didn't call and Moma put me on phone restriction 'cause I had the music playing too loud when she came home the other day."

"Oh, nothing much."

"Nothing much?! Did Mr. Smithey show up?" I could tell from his face he was hoping for some juicy gossip.

"No. Just Mr. Fred."

"Did you catch them 'getting it on?'"

"No! Mr. Fred just spent some time with Madame A and left."

"That's all?"

"That's all." *He's not ready for the hot tub story just yet.*

"I thought for sure ol' Smithey would be up in the mix. Maybe he called and Madame A told him she had company. Did he call since you been there?"

"Not that I know of. The only other person to come by was Aunt Brenda."

"She had Carla, Laquinsa and the little kids with her, didn't she?"

"Yeah. They're living with her now." I shake my head at the sad picture they created.

"They hadn't never really left. Every other week, one or the other is moving in or moving out."

"That's what Madame A said. You should have been there. She told them *off!*."

"She did? What did she say? Don't leave out nothing!" Weenie says, excitedly.

"She told them they needed to get out of Aunt Brenda's house and get their own place and help her out with money and stuff."

"Carla's too stingy to give up the Benjamins and I know she got some 'cause she always around town selling her food stamps."

"How do you know?"

"She tried to sell some to Moma one day. Moma asked her how she was gonna be selling food stamps when her kids were running around all the time asking anybody they know for food."

"Do they?" I ask, disbelief on my face.

"They beg *all* the time. Carla don't stop them or say nothing."

"That's a shame. Those kids gonna be locked up in 'Big Mary' if she don't do something about them now." Big Mary is what we call the state penitentiary.

"She ain't gonna do nothing about them 'cause she ain't doing nothing about herself."

"I know."

"Do you think Mr. Fred or Mr. Smithey gonna come back over there tonight? I'm gonna ask Moma if I can stay, if you think so."

"Weenie, I don't think so. Why don't you see if you can stay tomorrow night? Madame A's pretty tuckered out and all, so she might let you stay tomorrow."

"Shoot. Del, Moma was mad as a greased duck after you left. She stomped around the house throwing things and yelling. She even made me clean out the refrigerator!"

"You know how Moma is when she is mad. She's gonna make somebody pay and unfortunately, you were the only one there."

"You can say that again."

"Where's Daddy?"

"Working. You know he don't get home before night."

"I forgot." I change the subject. "I guess you ready to go back to school."

"Naw. I'm just ready to grow up and get on out of here. I'm sick of Yokel. Ain't nothing to do here at all."

"Well, you'll be there in a few years time. Don't rush it," I placate him.

"That's easy for you to say. You're already almost out of the house."

"What are y'all doing out here?!" the irritated voice of my mother rushes out to us and we jump.

"Ah...just talking. Y'all finished?" I answer quickly.

"Just about...oh, they finished. Let me speak to Moma, then we gonna go on home, Weenie."

My mother makes small talk as the people pass by her on the way to their cars. She takes Madame A's arm and helps her down the steps and to the car.

"Mama, you go home and lie down," my mother instructs as they reach the car.

"Lena, I'm going home and do just that."

Moma looks at me. "Del, now Mama don't need no company tonight. You just tell anybody calling or stopping by she's—"

"Lena, let me be the judge of that!" Madame A snaps.

"Well, you *don't*. Fred don't need to be up there as soon as you get out of the hospital. You need your rest," Moma insists, her spine rigid.

"And I'm getting my rest! Ain't nothing wrong with folks checking on an old woman. You need to quit being so stiff. As tight as you keep your behind, it's a wonder Andy hadn't taken up with half the county!" Madame A says, her finger in Moma's face.

"Mama!" My mother exclaims, sudden fury contorting her features. "You've got no call to be talking like that to me! Andy ain't complained in all this time and I don't reckon he will. Anyway, I'm not the one got pulled down in the street by some men!"

"I didn't get pulled down, I slipped on a rock."

"Whatever."

Oh no! Madame A hates whenever somebody says 'whatever' to her.

"Don't you *say* 'whatever' to me! You just run things over at your house and I'll run things over at mine. Del, let's go." Madame A finishes and turns her head away from my mother.

"Uh...Bye, Moma, Weenie," I say slowly, feeling pulled between the two women.

"Bye, Del," Weenie replies alone since my mother is practically stomping her way to the car.

I help Madame A into the car. Things are quiet as we drive home and enter the house.

"Del, I'm just gonna go on to bed. You stay up as late as you want."

"You want anything before you go?"

"No. I've had just about all the excitement I can handle for one day."

"Good night, then."

"Good night, baby."

CHAPTER

10

I manage to rise before Madame A the next morning. By the time she strolls into the kitchen, I have the sausage cooked, the eggs in the skillet and the toast in the oven. She grunts when she sees me.

"You know, you don't have to get up this early just for me. Usually, I just grab a bowl of oatmeal in the morning."

"You're not hungry?" I ask, looting at the food I'd prepared.

"Not really. I'm not used to nobody being here cooking for me, so I would hate to get used to it and then you go on back to school."

"I've still got the better part of the week, so just enjoy my breakfast for now."

"You put on any tea?" She looks at the stove.

"I've got the water boiling in the kettle right now."

"Good. I could use a cup."

"Let me get these eggs out and I'll fix you one." I find the cups, place a tea bag in one and pour the hot water over it. Dipping it slowly until the tea bag is steeped enough, I sit the cup gingerly in front of her.

She blows on the hot liquid before sipping it slowly. "Thank you baby. I always need a little something in the morning."

"I see you prefer tea over coffee. Why is that?"

Placing the cup on the mat, she says, "Well, Americans drink a lot of coffee, but the rest of the world drinks tea. Hot tea. I found that out when your granddaddy and me were traveling all over world."

"That's interesting."

"Shucks, they didn't even know what iced tea was. You should have seen how the folks looked at me when I put ice in that hot tea," she said, chuckling again.

"Really?"

"Yes. Child, if you don't do anything else in life, try to travel some. You'll be surprised at how folks do things in the rest of the world. A lot of folks around here never go anyplace really. Going to Jackson is a big deal to them, and that's only an hour and a half away. They think going to New Orleans—two hours driving—is going on vacation."

Thinking about the people in Yokel, I reply, "Yeah, they do."

"I'm telling you, if folks would travel out of their own holes more, they would find out there's other ways of doing things."

"Where all did you and Grandpa Edgar travel to?" I asked, intrigued with their life.

"We started out in Paris, then he got transferred to Japan, and later on, Brazil."

"Wow! Which place did you like best?"

"Oh, I don't know. Paris was pretty open to black folks. They thought we were exotic or something since Josephine Baker had already taken the town by storm. The Japanese folks just left us alone. They hadn't never really seen any colored people before and I think they were scared of us. Now, Brazil had it going on! Those folks sure know how to have a good time. The only way you could tell I wasn't one of them was by my accent. We enjoyed ourselves there."

"How did Grandpa die?" I ask, curious.

Her face saddens. Sitting still, she takes a moment before she says, "We'll, Edgar got sick with malaria. We think he must have picked it up in Brazil or maybe overseas. He just got down and the medicine didn't help him at all. I tried all the doctors that would treat our people until there were no more. He died one night, about three months after your mama was born."

"She never really knew him, did she?" I ask quietly.

"No. She never got a chance."

"Do you think that's why she is the way she is?" I ask, thinking how they blame almost *everything* on the father not being in the home today.

"I don't think so. Your mother has been bossy and judgmental all her life. She was trying to tell Maynard and Brenda what to do when she was just a little gnat."

"She still does."

"Yeah. They don't pay her no mind, though. She's still gonna interfere in everybody's business."

"Right. Madame A...you mentioned that the white man in the photo might have Mr. Smithey when he was young."

"Yes."

"You were seeing him before now?" I ask, hoping she wouldn't be offended.

"Me and Smithey been seeing each other off and on for many years. In between my marriages and even while he was still married."

"Oh!" I say shocked. I knew Madame A liked men, but I had no idea she would go with married men.

"Don't be surprised, girl. Life throws people together all the time. You can't always wait until the timing is perfect. You got to try to help things along sometimes. When me and Smithey would run into each other and feel that old longing, we just did what felt good at the time."

"But—"

"Oh, I know it sounds wild, but I ain't never been one to see just a person's color. I don't know where I got that from, 'cause I've been called names just like every other colored person, but I don't. I believe you might miss your next 'good thing,' trying to wait on the 'perfect thing.'"

"Yeah. I see what you mean." And I did. Many women probably missed a having a good time waiting for the Prince when the Knight was really the one for them anyway. "Did you know him growing up?"

"No. Colored and white children didn't play together or nothing back then. If you saw a white person, you gave them plenty of room and hoped they didn't notice you. Just terrible how some of them acted towards us. We're people, just like them. We go to work, have families, and worry about giving our children a good life, too. Why they're always thinking they better than us, I don't know."

I remembered the few incidents I'd had with discrimination. The episodes always left me furious, wanting to cry out, 'Why are you acting like this? You don't even know me. Why I always gotta be called the

'N' word?' But, I usually ignored their hate-filled words, even though my blood was boiling and shame flooded my body.

"Anyway, Smithey's folks owned the newspaper and I worked at the print shop next door. See, I came home after Edgar died and I lived off what little we had saved, but after a year, the money was gone and I had to feed my children somehow. The man at the printing shop offered me a job cleaning at first. I didn't want to take it, but I needed some money bad. After he learned that I corrected copy pretty good, he started letting me help with the flyers and church bulletins he printed. Oh, I still cleaned at little, but mostly, I checked the copy before he set the type."

"Mr. Smithey started liking you then?"

"Not right away. Afterall, he just saw me as the maid that worked next door. One day, he came over and my boss was out, so we started talking about little things. When he found out I'd been to places he only *hoped* to go, he started seeing me in a different light."

"I'll bet he did." Madame A was definitely not the norm for these parts.

"Anyway, he began coming over more and more, whenever he could get a break, to talk to me. We became fast friends. My boss started noticing how often he was over there and said something to his daddy, though.

Smithey was called on the carpet about our friendship. I heard him and his daddy arguing through the walls. It was terrible. But, Smithey still kept coming over like nothing was wrong and that's when I knew he was different from the other folks around here."

"So did y'all hook up then?" I wiggle with excitement.

"No. I saw the writing on the wall and I put together a resume and sent it off to some of those newspapers and magazine in New York, Chicago and Boston. I'd gotten good with writing by helping Edgar out with his assignments and all. When I got a reply from *The Colored People's Digest*, I gave my notice and hopped on a train to Chicago."

"Just like that?"

"Just like that. I wasn't trying to cause my folks no trouble or shame again, so I left the kids with them and took off at the first opportunity. My mother's sister in Chicago let me stay with her."

"How long did they have to stay with your parents?"

"Well, I thought it would only be a few months, until I got settled and all, but, the magazine sent a bunch of us to Liberia to check on the 'Back to Africa' movement. With the long ship ride over, covering the assignment for nearly a year, and the ship ride back, it was almost two years before I saw my children. You mama acted like she hardly knew me. I tell you nothing has cut me deeper than the way she acted when I got home." Pain etches Madame A's face.

"I'll bet. So, you and Mr. Smithey got together then?"

"For a little while. But, we still couldn't go to a motel or nothing together, so it was kind of hard. Smithey's folks had a cabin up on the other side of Hazlehurst, so he would take me there when we could, but that wasn't too often. After that Thumper incident, I was real careful about where I went and who might be there. It wasn't too common to see a white man and black woman riding together, so we saw each other in snatches."

"That must have been hard. Do you love him?"

"I fancied that I was in love with him at one time, but some things we both did later changed our feelings for each other a little."

"Like?"

"Well for one, I got married to Timothy Whitehead, one of the men that went on assignment to Liberia for the magazine. Smithey wanted to marry me, but we couldn't. So, I thought my kids needed a 'father figure' and I set out to find them a good daddy."

"He got married too, didn't he?"

"Yeah, but after I did."

"How long were you and Mr. Whitehead married?" I ask, feeling disembodied from this step-grandfather I'd never even known.

"Not even three years. Now, that's one time I bought some common sense."

"What do you mean?"

"My mama always said, 'Ain't no sense like bought sense.' I didn't know what she meant until I was married to Tim. Smooth as ice cream on the outside, that man had a heart like metal."

"He was mean to you and the kids?"

"Was he? Things started out good, mind you, but after the first year, I noticed that he was drinking all the time and he started swatting the kids for any little thing. I held my tongue about the drinking, but when he started hitting my kids, I said no way, brother. We started fighting regularly and he began staying out later and later. Finally, he lost his job at the magazine, since he missed so much time drinking and stumbling around the streets of Chicago."

"That must have been awful!"

"It was. I'm trying to work and raise kids and his butt just sat around the house everyday doing nothing. Didn't lift a finger to have dinner cooked or straighten up the house or anything. Now, I tried to encourage him and help him find work, but the minute I found him a job, he found any little reason to quit—they talked to him like he was a child, the job was beneath him...anything. On top of that, he was sneaking money out of my purse for booze and had a nasty attitude when I asked him about it. The kids had started tiptoeing around the house, trying not to set him off. After another year and a half, I finally woke up. My kids had fear in their eyes every time he was around and the only times they laughed was when they were with me by myself. I'd had enough, so I told him I was divorcing him."

"What did he do when you told him that?" I already knew men didn't handle rejection well.

"Oh, he got loud and said some really mean things about me and the kids. He acted like he was gonna get violent, but I told him that if he lifted a *finger* towards me, we were gonna be front page news the next day."

"Did you divorce him? I thought he died?" I ask for clarification.

"Oh, he died. He stormed out the house after I'd said my piece. He was already drunk, so I guess in his anger, he didn't see the bus coming down the street and stepped out in front of it."

"Oh, no!" I squeal.

"Yes."

"That must have made you feel guilty."

"Not in the least. Sometimes, when folks treat you real bad, you can't allow yourself to feel sorry for them. They dish out evil and finally evil catches up to them. Now, the one good thing that did come about was the $10,000 life insurance money. I'd kept paying on his policy even though he wasn't giving me a red cent and I got a blessing for my efforts! Girl, I kissed that insurance agent when he passed me the envelope with that check in it. That's like $50,000 today."

"Dog, that's was a lot of money."

"Still is. I bought us a house and put the rest in savings bonds."

"How long did you live in Chicago?"

"About another five years. The neighborhood where we lived started changing. The kids weren't nice to the grown ups anymore and gangs were sprouting up everywhere. Then, I started realizing that the folks hanging around the streetlights were selling drugs. When Maynard came home with a gang symbol tattooed on his forearm, I liked to have killed him. I knew then that something had to change or my baby would end up like all the hollow-eyed druggies I was seeing on the streets or worse, dead. I sold that house for what I could get and dragged the kids back down here to Yokel."

"What did they say when you told them you were moving?"

"Wasn't nothing to be said. I bought the tickets and made them go to the train station," Madame harrumphs.

"Uncle Maynard didn't give you any trouble?"

"He tried, but I tell you, I was at my snapping point with him. When he mouthed off and snatched his arm from me, I beat his ass good! I just *lost* my mind. I couldn't believe that this child of mine had the *nerve* to lift his hands towards me. Who had been feeding him?" she asks, anger reddening her face. "I tore his ass up! Nearly *broke* his arm. The next morning when I said 'Let's go,' he got in the taxi with no trouble at all."

"Then y'all just came on back to your folk's house?"

"Yeah. My parents were old. My daddy had sugar and Mama was feeling poorly all the time. My other sisters and brothers had moved away, so nobody was there to help take care of them and the farm. Pearl, bless her soul, came back and helped me again."

"You just jumped right in?"

"Sure did. My daddy had 200 acres of prime land and it was killing him trying to keep everything going. He owed back taxes and he was too proud to ask his kids for help. I cleared up those taxes when I found out and begin farming with him."

"But did the kids know anything about farming?"

"Not much. They remembered a little from the time they lived there before, but I showed them the rest. I bought a good bull and bred it with the cows we already had, kept the good heifers and sold the rest. I planted a big garden—those kids know they hated when I told them we were going to the garden—and fed my folks and some other ones too. Just when it looked like things were gonna work out, my daddy drops dead of a heart attack."

"No!"

"Yes. Mama was so heartbroken, that she got down and died within a year."

"That must have been awful!" Just the thought of losing Moma and Daddy chilled my spine.

"Girl, that was the worse time of my life. When your mother and father die... ain't no words for that pain. Anyway, I had to raise my kids. Maynard was almost out of school and he had turned himself around and wanted to go to college. Brenda was still in high school and your mother was just out of elementary school. I couldn't just roll over and forget about the living. So, I just sucked it up and went through the motions until the pain lessened a little."

BRRRIIINNNGGG!

I quickly answer the phone.

"Hello."

"Yes. Is Ms. Adoll available?" the voice of an older, obviously white man asks.

"Yes sir, she is." I hand the phone to my grandmother.

"Hello?"

"Hello, yourself..."Madame A says, her voice suddenly bright.

"Nothing..."

"Hmmm, what time?"

"That's fine. I'll see you then," she finishes and hand the phone to me.

"Who was that?" I ask.

"Smithey."

"Is he coming over?"

"Later on this afternoon. He wants to take me out to dinner."

Mr. Fred one night and Mr. Smithey tonight? Madame A dates more than me!

"What time he supposed to be here?"

"Oh, around seven. We're gonna eat some Chinese food over in Brookhaven."

"Chinese food! I didn't know you liked Chinese food." Madame A surprises me more and more every day.

"Baby, I eat almost anything, except those nasty oysters. When I was working and traveling, I got a chance to try out just about every kind of cuisine on the face of the earth—Italian, Chinese, Japanese, Indian, West Indian, Mexican—you name it and I have probably tried it at least once."

"Madame A you are a trip! Whatcha' wearing tonight?"

"I don't know. I was thinking about that nice black and white Jersey outfit you and Weenie bought me for Christmas, but I think it's too dressy. Sluggish as I feel, I may just put on that new windsuit I picked up at McRae's last month. It looks good, but not overdressed. As long as Smithey doesn't show up in a tie and coat, I should be all right."

Running a hand through her hair, she says, "Oh Lord, I forgot about my hair. The steam from the hot tub made every, last one of my curls disappear. Del, can you wash it and put some curls in it for me? This broke arm gonna make it hard for me to work with it myself and I don't feel like sitting up at the beauticians for half the day."

"Sure. I've got a blow dryer and some curling irons in my bag. Let me get them and turn 'em on."

"I've got a few of my own under the bathroom cabinet. I'm gonna take a bath and then I'll let you work on it. We got time. He won't be here until seven. Let's just eat this good breakfast for now. Oh, I need to go into town to pick up a few things and have the doctor check my arm again."

"We can go after we finish eating."

"That sounds fine." With that she digs a fork into a sausage and pops it into her mouth.

CHAPTER

11

The downtown area looks sleepy as we coast along Main Street. There were few cars in front of the stores so I was able to find a parking space with little trouble. As I helped Madame A from the car, a voice calls out to her.

"Miss Doll! Miss Doll! I heard you had been in the hospital," a gruff male voice says.

Turning her head, she slips on a wide grin as she views the man. Short, bald and wearing a three piece suit with a straw hat, he looked like a Bahama lawyer or something.

"Boomer Lett! When did you get into town?" she asks before being engulfed in broad arms.

"I got in a few days ago. Moma said she saw you at choir practice. I'd hope to see you, but I didn't really know. You know after the last time we saw each other, I wasn't sure if I was welcome." *What happened the last time they say each other?*

"Boomer, you're always welcome at my house. I'm the queen in it and I say who comes and goes up there."

"Still fiesty, as always," Boomer replies with a grin and another hug. Keeping his hands wrapped around her, he whispers something in her ear. Madame A guffaws loudly in return.

"Quit! You're bad, Boomer," she says, swatting at his chest.

"Only for you, Miz Doll. Only for you," he replies with a mischievous look in his eyes.

Laughing again, Madame A finally notices me. Clamping down on her laugher and clearing her throat, she says, "Boomer, this is my granddaughter, Delphine. She's Lena's girl. Del, this is Boomer Lett, Miz June's son."

"How you doing?" Boomer says, nodding at me. "You the spitting image of your Mama. How is she?"

"Fine," I reply.

"I went to school with your Uncle Maynard. I spent many a day over there at the farm with them."

"Sure did and near 'bout ate me out of house and home."

"That's 'cause you cooked so good. Think I could get a taste of some of your cooking before I leave on Saturday?"

147

"I don't know. This arm got me laid off from cooking so Del's been over there cooking and helping me out. I might be able to get Maynard over to barbecue though."

"Don't do nothing special on my occasion. I'll just stop by and sit and talk one of these nights."

"You do that. You still with your wife?"

Boomer smiles as he replies, "No indeed. She wanted a city man and I was just a little too 'country' for her taste. She couldn't refine me enough to suit her and her folks so we split up over a year ago."

"Probably for the best. After the one time I saw her, I knew you had trouble on your hands. I tell you if that gal held her nose any higher, she would drown when it rained."

"Sure would. Anyway, I'm a bachelor and on the lookout for a good woman. Know any?" His eyes twinkle as he asks Madame A this.

"Now you know I don't play Cupid for nobody. When the mess goes bad, the first thing y'all gonna do is cuss me behind my back. When you find somebody, good or bad, it's gonna be without my help."

"You're right, too. So, you haven't got married on me, have you?"

"No. I'm just gonna date until I die. Since my last husband passed, I just don't have the taste for no permanent man around the house."

"You know, a man *does* come in handy around the house sometimes."

"Anything I need doing, I got children and grandchildren to help me. If they're not available or can't do it, I'll hire someone. I don't need to put up with all the rest of that mess just for no handyman around the house."

"What about just for good old companionship?"

"Didn't I tell you I date? I get companionship whenever I want it."

"Some *steady* companionship."

"It's steady enough for me. Anyhow, I'm too old for marriage."

"You ain't too old, you just set in your ways."

"And don't want to get set in nobody else's. Leave me alone, Boomer, I'm fine."

"You sure are. I'm gonna run over to the store and get some things for Mama. I'll be stopping by before I leave."

"See that you do. Bye now."

"Ladies." He tips his hat.

Turning back to me, I ask Madame A what had happened the last time he was home.

"Well, he got into that 'ignant oil' and said some pretty strong things to his high-falluting wife while we were having a cookout over to my house with family and friends. You were visiting your college for High School day and a football game that weekend so you missed it. It must have been about thirty folks over there when he decided to act a fool. That gal pissed Boomer off so *bad* that he grabbed her shirt and tore it off her back! You should have seen her running around holding her hands over her chest."

"Really?" I say, hardly able to believe that a *husband* would actually pull his wife's clothes off in front of other people.

"Yes. I got so tickled 'cause she had been up there looking her nose down on everything, that I just couldn't lift a hand to help her. Your mother was ready to kill Boomer, but I intervened before she could bust him up sides the head. Somebody finally gave that gal a towel or something to put on, but the damage had been done. She cussed us *all* before she left in their car."

"Madame A, you are terrible!" I meant it, too.

"Maybe, but that gal was acting pretty blue-blooded towards us the whole afternoon. You'd have thought we were just off the boat from Africa or something."

"But, pulling her shirt off of her? That ain't right."

"I didn't say it was. I said I was tickled when it happened. Besides, that was between her and Boomer. Now if Maynard had done it, I might have acted differently."

"I'll *bet*." I say, unconvinced.

"Why don't we just change this conversation. I need to go to Bill's and then over to the grocery store for some breakfast food."

"Okay."

A small red sports car zooms down the center of the street. Slowing down at the caution light, it beeps then continues on.

"Who was that?" I ask.

"Monroe Blackjack"

"Reverend Blackjack's grandson?"

"Yep."

Everything Weenie said came back to me. "Ah...I heard that he and y'all's piano player got something going on."

"Maybe they do," Madame A replies nonchalantly.

"You don't care?"

"One thing I learned in life, folks gonna talk about you whether you doing what they say you're doing or not, so you might as well be happy. If they like it, I love it. I just hope they're careful. Folks get crazy when they run into 'those kind' of men around here."

"Reverend Blackjack hadn't tried to stop them or anything?" I ask, incredulous. Preachers *are* supposed to do that, right?

"Black ain't the one to be trying to tell nobody what to do. I've been trying to get him moved for years, but the rest of the folks won't back me."

"Does he really have some children with women in the church?"

"That's what they say. I *do know* that Carla's baby, Tralph, look a *whole lot* like some of Black's kids."

"What?!" *Carla and Reverend Blackjack?*

"Girl, why're you surprised? Carla is what we refer to as a 'money ho.' She'll spread wide for anybody showing her a little money. I know that's my granddaughter, but she ain't right at all. Shoot, I've seen the way Black looks at her and talks to that boy...something's going on more than Bible school. Look, Black has done it and got away with it before and he gonna keep on doing it until Barbara puts her foot down. She messed up when she didn't do nothing after she found out about the first one. Now she can hardly hold her head up. She's scared to speak to any of the women at church, 'cause she don't know *who* he might be tapping this week."

I just stand there shaking my head. Reverend Blackjack is worse than worse. When are people gonna quit following the hypocrites in the pulpit?

"Well, that's their business. I just hope Carla ain't playing games and calling over to that woman's house. Women might be able to take a lot when it's out in the streets, but when you start bringing the mess to the house, you talking cemetery shit then."

"I hope Carla doesn't do that."

"She's trifling enough to, but rest assured, if she does, I'm sure we'll hear about it. Let's get out of this heat. We can talk in Bill's just as well as the street."

The cool air of Bill's Dollar Store refreshes us. Madame A finds the items she needs quickly and we head over to the grocery store. Getting the breakfast food, I watch Madame A speak and flirt with every man she meets—the manager, the delivery men and the baggers. The few women in the store seem to acknowledge her with reluctance. In fact, we saw Miss Easter Chaps and she rolled her eyes and sucked at her bad fitting dentures, but she didn't say a word. This didn't seem to even faze Madame A and she spoke to all of them anyway. Loading our groceries in the car, Madame A talks to two other men that happen to be passing before getting into the car for the drive home.

"Madame A, why do the women always act like that around you?"

"Chile, they've been acting like that for years. I guess they're are jealous or something."

"Some, maybe, but all of them?" It's dangerous to have a bunch of women mad at you.

"Baby, I don't know what goes on in their heads. All I do know is, I'm free and single and I'll talk to anybody I want to. If they have a problem with me speaking with their men, then they need to tell them not to speak to me. Del, you'll kill yourself worrying about other folks. The only folks you *ever* need to be worried about are the ones taking care of you. Last time I looked in the mirror, I saw the person taking care of me and that was *me*," Madame A says, pointing the finger of her good hand to her chest.

"I got it."

"Let me get this arm checked and then we can get on back so you can do my hair in time for my date."

CHAPTER

12

Time flies as I wash, dry and wait to curl Madame A's hair while she watches her favorite soap operas. Mundane tasks of laundry and straightening up the house take up more time. Before either of us realizes it, 4 o'clock is almost upon us.

Shifting Madame A into high gear takes a good deal of encouragement since she is still groggy from her afternoon nap. However, once she shifts, she is a flurry of activity—bathing, powdering, perfuming and fussing over what to wear. Deciding, *finally*, on the wind suit, she settles down to wait for her date close to 6:00.

BBRRRRIINNNGGG!

I answer the phone, hoping that it was *not* that Bertha person again. "Hello?"

"Yes. Is Miss Adoll available?" The same male voice from this morning asks.

"Yes she is. Can you please hold?"

"Yes."

"Madame A, I think Mr. Smithey's on the phone for you."

"Well, hand it over, child."

Passing the phone to her eager hands, I perch on the sofa arm to stay in reach to retrieve the phone, as well as eavesdrop on the conversation.

"Hello, Smithey..."

"Really?"

"Uh hum...."

"That sounds good. You still coming at seven?"

"Great. I'll see you then."

Taking the phone from her outstretched hands, I ask, "So, what did Mr. Smithey want? Y'all still going out?"

"Yes, indeed. He wants to take me over to McComb to see a new play after we eat, so he's gonna be here a little earlier."

"Oh. What time do you think you will be back?"

"It's gonna be late. Hey, why don't you stay at your mama's tonight? I would hate to leave you out here all by yourself and since it looks like we'll be pretty late, I would feel better if you stayed at your house tonight."

"You sure? I could get Weenie to come over here with me." *I don't want to go home!*

"No. Weenie ain't no protection if something happens. It might be best if you just stayed with your folks. Yes, that's the best thing," she states with finality.

"All...right," I reply hesitantly. "You know Moma is gonna act up something *awful* when I go home tonight, don't you?"

"Ah, shit! Call the *po*-lice! Lena's mama's gone on a date!" Madame A exclaims, her arms flung into the air like she had just felt a touch of the Holy Ghost. "Girl, I told you folks are gonna act like they're gonna act. Your Mama needs to let me alone. I ain't over there trying to run her house, so why she think she gonna run mine?"

"You know how she is—"

"Sure do...stiff as a paint-dried brush. I wish she would realize that I'm not married to nobody. I'm not *cheating* on nobody. Ain't *nobody* cheating with me. I'm *available*. If she can't deal with that...too bad, so sad."

"Aw, Madame A, Moma just thinks you are moving too fast with your arm and all still in the cast."

"Girl, I ain't getting no younger! If I sit around here waiting for this old arm to heal, I might be dead before I get my next date!"

"She just thinks that two men at your...*age*, is a bit much."

"No. Your Mama thinks that two men at *any age* is too much. I'll give her this, when she was dating—the

little she did before she got swept off her feet by Andy—
she stuck to one fella like a cootie. She wasn't gonna look
or talk to nobody when she had a 'boyfriend' *unless* it
was family."

"I believe that."

"It's true. Your Mama's been straight-laced and
conservative all her days. I use to think she was trying to
be exactly how I wasn't. I don't know…she needs to
lighten up a little." Chuckling, she continues, "Your
Mama is a one-man woman through and through. She's
got her man and she's happy. I believe Tammy Wynette
wrote that song, 'Stand By Your Man' just for her, cause
Lena's gonna stand, lean, sway and lay down for Andy."

"She's not!"

"Yes she is! The sun rises and sets around Andy
for her. Oh, she loves you and your brother, but Andy
runs her motor. Shoot! If anything happens to your
daddy, you can bet when she dies, they ain't gonna get
nothing but a huge pile of dust when they pull off her
drawers at the funeral home." Madame A finishes,
slapping her hands on her plump thighs for emphasis.

"Quit!"

"Girl, that's the truth!"

"But isn't that the way it's supposed to be?"

"Well, I guess that's how we're supposed to *hope* it is. It's just that the real thing don't always go like we planned."

"I know."

"Sometimes, the folks you marry tell you they love you with one hand and slap the fire out of you with the other. Sometimes, they claim they can't live without you, but poke in every woman's panties they can. Sometimes, they know you need stuff in your house, but spend it out in the streets before they get home. I'm not saying you shouldn't wish for the perfect relationship, it's just that when something happens that blindsides you, if you are caught up in a fairy tale, you'll find yourself floundering and a lot of women I know never recover from it."

"Really?" I ask, disconcerted about what she just said.

"Just go down to the nursing home. I know plenty of those women down there. Children gone and they put their last into their man. When he either died or left them, they just went down. It's hard to find a man who will marry a woman with a bunch of kids and trying to raise kids and work runs you down, so you look a mess most of the time. By the time the kids are gone, the woman has made one of two choices—either she constantly ran around looking for a man, ignoring her kids, or she focused on her kids and ignored men. She can't do both well. Either way, if she has found a man, her kids won't like him or there won't be any available men for her if she waits."

"You make it sound so...bad."

"Sometimes life is. You've got to learn to make your own happiness. It don't come bottle up in a pair of boxer shorts. A man is supposed to *enhance* the happiness you already have, not be the root or sometimes the *death* of it."

"But when I find somebody I like, that's when I feel the happiest." I didn't mean to say this but the words just blurt from my mouth.

"And you're gonna feel sad and depressed when it's over *unless* you realize that that man is just passing through, helping you to get stronger. Men ain't promised. Ain't nowhere it's written that a man that promises to love, honor and be faithful, gonna do just that. Now when you know who *you* are already, you can handle these types of things. Not go off the deep end and cry, lose weight and think about suicide."

"Yeah, I know a lot of girls that act like that. Why is it like that for us?"

"That's the way we've been programmed—you ain't a woman if you can't get a man. Lies passed on from mothers to daughters for generations. Don't matter if the man treats you like sewer slime, you've got to have a man. We're supposed to ignore what we want 'cause what the man wants is more important. It can be the color of the wallpaper or where you're gonna live, we're supposed to give in to what the man wants, 'cause if you don't, he might leave you and that is worser than worse." Madame A sucks at her teeth.

"That's not right!"

"Del, right is a direction or what you do with a pen and paper. There ain't no 'right' rules in a relationship. There is a 'correct' or better way and a wrong way to do things, but there is no right."

"So you are saying, I've got to learn to be happy with *me* as I *am* before I can hope to find happiness with someone else."

"Yep. You've got to bring something to get something in return," she nods.

"That's deep."

"Sho' is. Fred didn't call did he? I forgot he said he might want to do something today. Oh well, like they say, 'the early bird catches the worm.'"

"What if he shows up before Mr. Smithey does?"

"He'll just have made a trip for nothing then, won't he?" Madame giggles loudly.

Madame A is a hoot! She might *need* to get a man schedule as busy as she is.

The sound of a car pulling into the driveway intrudes into our conversation. Rising, I quickly open the door, hoping we hadn't talked Mr. Fred up. I sigh in relief as an antique roadster, driven by a white-haired Smithey Zacharias, pulls to the door.

I hadn't seen Mr. Smithey in years so I was saddened to see that time had changed him so much. I remember him as a smiling, chubby white man with wavy brown hair that always gave us candy. Today, he is still smiling and chubby, but wrinkles have crowded around his face and neck, giving him a "warbler" appearance. He sees me and waves and I wave back. Exiting the car, he limps to the door and greets me.

"Hello, young lady. I'm Smithey Zacharias and you are?"

"Delphine Andrews, but my grandmother calls me Del."

"Del! How are you? You've grown up so much I didn't recognize you. I should have known, though. You look so much like your grandmother in her younger days."

"Thank you, sir."

"What are you doing now? Aren't you in college?"

"Yessir. I'm a freshman this year."

"That's good. What are you majoring in?"

"Pre-med."

"Pre-med. That's a pretty competitive field there. You planning to come back here and practice when you finish up everything?"

"I don't...know. I haven't really thought that far down the line. I'm just trying to get through Biology 102 right now."

"Well, that understandable. Just consider coming home when you're finished. You can live just as good here as in a big city plus, you don't have the crime and traffic and you can—"

"Smithey Zacharias you gonna talk the ears off of that gal! Come on up in here!" Madame A pushes past me to grab his hand and pull him forward.

"Adoll, me and Del are just getting reacquainted. I haven't seen her since she was a little thing. Del, do you remember me giving you candy every time you all came past the shop?" He turns to me and says.

"Yes, I do." *Now I know why.*

"Smithey gave y'all so much candy, I thought I was gonna have to get you fitted for dentures before you turned ten," Madame A giggles.

"Oh, Adoll. I just love to see kids happy, that's all."

"I know."

Mr. Smithey takes a moment to survey Madame A. "Look at you! Adoll, you look good enough to spread butter on and eat."

"You're too much, Smithey."

"You look real nice, Adoll," he responds in a warm voice.

"You don't look too bad yourself." They stand there staring at each other like long-lost lovers.

I clear my throat, causing them both to remember I was still in the room, in case they planned to say anything I didn't need to hear.

"Oh. I guess we can reminisce while we ride. You ready to go, Adoll?"

"Been ready."

"Alright then. You'd better get a scarf. I've got the top down."

"You gonna have me looking like a wild woman before we get there!"

"You want me to put it up?" Mr. Smithey asks, concern in his voice.

"Don't you dare. You know I like that convertible." Turning to me, Madame A say, "Del, you go ahead of us. I don't want to leave you up in here."

Grabbing my keys, I hug Madame A and walk to my car. As I pull out, I see Mr. Smithey settling her into the convertible, a loud pink scarf wrapped around her hair. I turn my attention to the road and the sudden dread I feel at the scene just waiting to be played out at my house.

CHAPTER

13

Anxiety coats my body as I pull into the driveway. I don't see Moma's car so I'm hoping she's not home. Weenie walks out of the house just as I reach the porch.

"Hey, Del. Where's Madame A?"

"On a date with Mr. Smithey. Moma home?"

"Naw. Somebody needed something, so she left to do something or another. I don't know what, though. So, ol' Smithey finally showed up. Why can't I be where the action is instead of cooped up over here with nothing to do?"

"Ain't no action over at Madame A's house. I imagine once Moma gets home and finds out she's out with Mr. Smithey, we're gonna have more action than we want." *Way* more.

"Yeah. She's gonna be plenty pissed when she hears this."

"Tell me about it. I started to circle back and just stay at the house anyway, but Moma made me a little scared about staying out there and folks being able to look in the house, Madame A having no curtains and all."

"Girl, I could have stayed out there with you," Weenie asserts.

"I told Madame A that, but she said you wouldn't be any protection if something happened."

"No *protection*? I'll bust a cap in *anybody's* behind we don't know! I ain't scared of *nothing*!" Weenie insists, his chest puffed out with bravado.

"Nothing but Moma."

"I ain't scared of Moma. I just don't want to get her mad. But I ain't *scared* at all."

"Yeah. We got any ice cream?" I ask, tired of this conversation.

"Naw. I finished off the last of it an hour ago."

"Weenie! Why'd you always eating up the last of the ice cream?" His second favorite food is ice cream. A carton of it is not safe in our house.

"I didn't know we were saving it. The store is still open. We can drive to town and get some if you want."

"You sure Moma won't be mad?"

"I'll just leave her a note and she'll be fine."

"Let's go then." Weenie runs into the house to leave the note and returns quickly.

"I'm ready."

We pile back into the car for the drive to town. Passing two pretty teen-age girls on matching red and blue bikes, Weenie leans out the window and yells out some mannish comments.

"Stop that! You're gonna get your fool head knocked off leaning out the window! Do you even *know* those girls?"

"Yeah. They go to my school. In fact, the one on the red bike is the girl that sent me that perfume you just *love*."

"You should be glad she didn't try to punch you in the face 'cause can't nobody like you sending you some mess that smells like that."

"That's what you think. I'm telling ya, I got the girls after me like ants at a picnic."

"Yeah, right."

I slow down and ride the shoulder of the road as a wide tractor passes. The driver of the tractor waves energetically at us. He looks familiar, but I can't really place him.

"Looks like your old flame is still interested."

"Who?" I ask, confused.

"You don't know who's driving that tractor?"

"No. Should I?" I say, staring at in the rear view mirror.

"That's Ray Ray Combs."

Ray Ray Combs. A name to evoke some memories there. Junior High prom. Homecoming Dance. First Love. The Other Girl. Me and Ray Ray had some fun before it all went South.

"*That's* Ray Ray?"

"Yeah. You didn't recognize him?"

"No. I thought he went to school over in Louisiana."

"He does. They must be on Spring Break just like you are."

"He sure looks different."

"You didn't know he had that bad wreck? It was right after Christmas. I must have forgotten to tell you about it. He broke his nose and had a lot of cuts to his face, so he looks a little different than he used to."

"Sure does. I had no idea that was Ray Ray."

"Well, now that he's seen you, he's probably gonna be hollering at you before you leave."

"He don't need to holler at me no more. Me and Ray Ray said *all* we needed to say before." The last thing I need is an old, dead-to-me flame trying to reignite the fire.

"Aw, don't be like that. I know you still care about him," Weenie chides me.

What in the world is he talking about? Ray Ray is just a bad memory that I've welded behind a DO *NOT*

169

OPEN UNLESS HE IS THE *LAST* MAN ON EARTH door. "Nope. I'm seeing somebody else at school."

"That Stefan guy you been talking about?" he asks, like I've haven't talked about Stefan a million times.

"Yeah."

"Didn't you say he was a junior?"

"Yeah."

"Uh hmmm," he says smugly.

"What?" I ask, wondering why he's acting this way.

"Now, think, what would a junior be doing with a freshman? I mean, he's *only* been out there two or three years. Don't you think he should have been able to find a 'steady' by that time? What's he doing cruising the freshman class?"

Why does he want to make me start thinking about things like this? Stefan has done nothing but treat me nicely. Well...mostly. True, he wants me to lose weight...but its only for my good and I usually see him only after dark, but after the talk with Madame A, I'm gonna change all that. "He had a girlfriend and it didn't work out."

"So he says. You sure the old girlfriend knows they ain't working out no more?"

"I haven't had any problems with her, so until I do, I'm gonna take him at him word."

"Sheesh!" Weenie slaps his forehead.

"What?" He doesn't even *know* Stefan.

"Nothing."

"I hate when you say 'nothing' like that. If you've got something to say, say it." I manage to get out between clenched teeth before I suddenly swerve to miss a dog running into the road.

"Whoa! You just watch the road and let's forget this conversation!"

"I *got* the road! I want to know what you are insinuating!" I shout, adrenaline surging through my system from the near miss and because he was asking all these stupid questions.

"Not a thing. I don't even know Stefan. If you say things are on the up and up, I believe you."

"Yeah, right. You're just like everybody else. 'Why would a junior be dating a freshman?' Why you think all men got to be dogs?"

"'Cause most guys are *especially* while they're young. I've been to campus to visit you and I would just about lose my mind trying to talk to all those fine mamas out there."

"That's you. You're not Stefan. He could have talked to any of them he wanted to. He just chose me."

Now what would Madame A say about this statement? *He* chose me. Why didn't *I* do the choosing? The more I talked and thought, the madder I was getting thinking about my "relationship" with Stefan.

"And I'm sure it will work out. Let's just get to the store before it closes. I want some Chocolate Swirl. What about you?" Weenie says, changing the direction of the conversation.

I feel deflated as an old balloon. I wearily reply, "I don't care. In fact, I'm not even in the mood for ice cream now."

"Don't be like that. I was just asking. What do I know about Stefan anyway?" he says, trying to brighten my suddenly down mood.

Just enough to make me start wondering about Stefan myself. "Just go on in and get something. Hurry up. You know Moma is gonna be home soon."

"Aw'ight." Weenie jumps out of the car and goes into the store.

I stare out the window feeling anxious and depressed. Is Stefan really being straight up with me or is he running the usual "game?" Yes, he has been out there a few years, but what's wrong with him liking a freshman? We are just talking about two or three years between us. That shouldn't make a difference or does it?

The things Madame A said about relationships and the realization that I recognized myself doing so many of those things, made my heart double-clutch.

Stefan only visits you at night.

He doesn't accept you as you are.

Why can't you guys walk around campus and act like a couple during the day?

He says he isn't into all those expressions of affection like holding hands or cuddling in broad daylight.

I could see the logic at the time, but now...I'm not so sure.

Make a joker live up to your standards.

Yes, that's what she said. What standards did I have for myself? I mean, it's true, I do plenty of stuff differently than I did at home, but I'm *not* at home. I always believed, 'When in Rome, act like the Romans.' I thought that if I acted like the other girls, then the guys would like me more. You know, see you when I see you. Be glad that he visits you at all. It's alright that he doesn't acknowledge our relationship when he's hanging out with his friends. Now...now I think maybe I've become a "no standards" girl. I'm taking whatever he dishes out, just because I want to have a "friend." And that's not even making the commitment to boyfriend. Just friend. Like it's a crime to say you really like one person. Seems like when you say "friend," you are keeping your options open. Is that what he's doing? More important, is that what I'm allowing him to do to me?

Weenie returns and stops my tangent of thought. "They didn't have Chocolate Swirl, so I got Butter Pecan. Think that will be alright?"

"It's fine, Weenie," I say, not really caring what kind of ice cream he got since I didn't feel like eating it anyway.

"So, Del, what do you and Madame A talk about? I mean, in between her getting visits from her boyfriends, don't you get bored over there sometimes?"

"Not really. Madame A has gone a lot of places and seen a lot of things. She talks about the things she's done and things people have done to her."

"Bad things?" Weenie asks quietly.

"Some…but Madame A has gotten a lot of wisdom from living, so I can't really say too many folks have treated her bad."

"She ever talked to you about Grandpa Edgar and her other husbands?"

"Yeah. She really misses Grandpa Edgar. You should have seen her face when she talked about him dying. I don't know if I'll ever find anybody I care about that much."

"Yes you will. We *all* will." Weenie states emphatically.

"Oh, now you've gotten wise in your young age?"

"Girl, I've always been wise for my age. That goofy stuff I do is just a front. I've got plenty of sense."

"And no relationship experience to speak about, so, what would you know about finding somebody to really love?"

"It's all in the stars, Del, it's all in the stars. There's a perfect 'soulmate' out there for each of us. We've just got to take our time and find him or her."

"Soulmates? You believe in that stuff?" I glance at Weenie to see if he's serious.

"Yeah. Don't you?"

"Not really. I always thought that if you lived your life right, then the right person would find you. But, is that the way it should be? I've got to admit, after talking with Madame A, it seems like I should be focusing on loving me before I can focus on loving somebody else."

"That seems like good advice. You listen to India Arie?"

"A little. She's had a good CD out a while back. Why?"

"I think you need to really listen to that cut about not being the average girl in a video. India Arie knows what she's talking about."

"I've jammed to the beat, but I can't say I've really listened to all the words."

"You need to check it out again. It might be what you need to hear."

"Look in the glove compartment. I think I've got the CD there."

Weenie rummages through the junk in the compartment until he locates the CD. Sliding it into the player, he selects the correct track. Soon, India Arie is pumping through the speakers. I slow down to focus on the words to the song.

When she begins singing about combing her head some days and others she didn't, I thought, Alright now. I can empathize with her.

My eyes start to sting when she sings about being a Queen. Say it! my heart yells. We are all Queens and we need to be treated like the Queens we are.

The misconception, mass deception stanza takes my breath away. After all, that's what Madame A said. Dang! Am I the last to hear this?

We are crawling now as I pump my arms in the air and holler out (messing the song up with the wrong words), feeling like I've just heard my new mantra. India is telling us women just how things are and how we are supposed to be.

As the song ends, I slam off my high and feel a wave of tears threatening. All the lies. The façades. The self-suppression and denial. For what? So we can fit somebody else's definition of us, not our own. I fan at my face, trying to stop the outburst I'm feeling, but a lone tear escapes and slowly draws a path down my cheek.

"You got it this time, didn't you, Del?" Weenie asks, not gloating or making fun, but with…appreciation in his eyes.

"I sure did, Weenie, I sure did."

Weenie nods his head slowly and stares at me, not speaking. I wrestle with my emotions. I want to bawl like a hungry baby, but I manage to control myself and hold in the sobs. After a few moments, he says, "Why don't you pull over at the next road? I can drive the rest of the way home."

"Just give me a few minutes. I'll be alright in a minute."

"You sure? I need the practice. Moma don't let me drive her too many places since I backed into that tree."

I started laughing in spite of my misery. The day my mother called and told me that Weenie managed to back into the *only* tree in the driveway, I just about peed in my pants. All the yard we got, and he hits the one, *huge* pine tree out front. I see why she doesn't let him drive much.

"That's all right. I *need* my car."

"Oh, you've got jokes."

"Nope. Just sense."

"Shut up."

I drive home with laughter ringing throughout the car as I rib Weenie over and over about his hitting the tree. Pulling into the yard, I see that my mother has returned home. This sobers us immediately.

"Well, the stuff is about to hit the fan," I say somberly.

"You can say that again."

Just as I stop the car, my mother walks out on the porch, hands on her hips. I see her glance into the car, then a pinched look mars her face.

"Hey, Moma," I call out.

"Hey, Del. Where's Mama or should I even guess?" My mother says, lips pinched.

"Well...she's gone out to dinner with Mr. Zacharias," I answer with trepidation.

"I should have known. What time you supposed to go back over there?"

"Uhm...she said she might be late, so I should stay over here tonight."

"She did, did she?" My mother's eyes narrow.

"Yes ma'am." I hold my breath. I was expecting a huge outburst at this point.

"So where y'all been?" my mother asks calmly, causing me to expel my breath in disbelief.

No outburst? No fussing?

"We've been to the store for some ice cream. Weenie ate it all up and we wanted to get some more," I manage to say, still watching her warily. That calmness might be a front. She's bound to show out any minute now.

"Uh hum. Weenie, did you get the storage room cleaned out like I told you?" she questioned, training her "mother's eye" on Weenie.

"Yes, Mama. I did it as soon as you left. Everything's neat and straight like you like it." Weenie bows dramatically for emphasis.

"Well, since you've already got dessert, why don't y'all just keep it up and make dinner too?"

"Aw Moma, you know Del don't cook like you do—"

"Who said Del was gonna be doing all the cooking? You're helping her."

"Me? Why…I—" Weenie stumbles along.

"—am glad you are gonna be cooking dinner. Y'all just wash your hands. I've got the greens on the

179

counter that you need to pick and cut up and I've pulled the roast out of the refrigerator. I want some potatoes with my roast and make sure that you make a little gravy too."

"You're not gonna help us?" Weenie asks in disbelief. He never was one for doing what he calls the "girlie" jobs around the house. Well, not before anyway.

"No. I'm just gonna sit out here and rest my mind. I've been over to Sister Lisa's house and her grandbaby has the croup so bad that nothing anybody does eases it. I'm just plumb tired from all that crying," Moma rubs her temple before she plops down into the rocking chair.

"All right. Well get right on that dinner, Moma. You just sit out here and we've got it in the kitchen." I say, nodding my head and bustling towards the door.

Weenie is just standing there with his mouth open so I grab his arm and push him in the house. Whatever has Moma in this mood, I'm glad we just got off with cooking dinner. I drag Weenie into the kitchen and wash my hands. He sits on the chair and stares up the hallway towards the door.

"Was that *our* mother?" Weenie asks, confusion all over his face.

"Yep. That was her."

"And we were worried for nothing."

"Just hold that thought. The night is still young." I didn't know how prophetic I was to become.

We commence to cook the dinner. After an hour in the hot kitchen, both of us are drenched in sweat from the heat of the oven and *sick* of smelling the food cooking. My mother never enters the house to check on us or anything. As the food nears completion, I wearily drag my sweaty body to the door and call her.

"Moma, the food is ready. You gonna come on in and eat now?"

"Y'all just go ahead. I'll be there in a minute," she tells me without looking back.

The sound of a car coming down the road makes us pause. The car nears the house and I can see that it is a late model BMW, one of those kinds you see on TV but never really hope to buy unless it's used. Music is booming as the car coasts into the yard, two heads bopping to the beat. The music suddenly stops and a figure hops out of the car and quickly shuts the door. I see that it is my uncle, Maynard. My mother stands, her face not changing at his arrival whatsoever. The other door opens and Boomer Lett gets out on the passenger side, almost falling in the process.

"Lena! How you doing!" my uncle says, walking quickly to the porch.

My Uncle Maynard is a lawyer in Clinton. A huge, dark man with a scar across his cheek (from a gang fight, *they say*, but I haven't asked), he has a roving eye for a pretty woman and a body that usually follows his eyes. His marriage is constantly on the rocks. It must be the money he makes that keeps Aunt Mary with him. I hear he manages to do pretty well with all the liability lawsuits.

"Well, look what the cat drug into the yard. What'chu doing down here?" Moma asks.

"I came down to check on Mama. I hadn't had a chance to before since I've been tied up in court. I went by the house and nobody was home so I thought she might be over here with you."

"Nope, she's not. Hello, Boomer," my mother says as Boomer bounds up the stairs like a happy puppy.

"Lena! You're still looking good. How 'bout giving me a hug?" he says, walking towards her to do just that.

"Get on 'way from me, Boomer. I'm still mad about how you treated your wife the last time you were here," she says huffily as she wrestles, futilely, to avoid the hug he is trying to give her.

"Girl, that's ancient history. Anyway, we ain't together no more. I'm a free man." Boomer replies, still trying to hug my mother.

"I'm still mad. What you two knucleheads doing riding around with the music so loud? Y'all still think y'all teenagers, don't you?"

"Well, we ain't old, that's for sure. Hey, Del. You got a hug for your young uncle?" That was a funny thought since my uncle has to be close to front side of sixty.

"Sure do." I say as I hug him tightly. I loved Uncle Maynard. He was such a clown, always doing anything to make me and Weenie laugh. "How long you staying?"

"Oh, probably tonight and tomorrow. Since I ran into Boomer, I might be having a little barbecue out at Mama's tomorrow."

"That sounds good."

Weenie walks out onto the porch. His eyes light up as he see Uncle Maynard. "Hey, Unc. What's up?" he asks, before hugging him briefly and doing the "man" handshake.

"Boy, I see Lena's still feeding y'all good. You must've grown a foot since I last saw you. The girls must be running you down."

"You know it. I got the girls after me like..." he stops as he notices Moma watching him closely, "...like a nice fella. A real *nice*, young fella."

Uncle Maynard chuckles. "I feel ya." He turns back to my mother. "Lena, you got a key to Mama's house? Me and Boomer want to head over there."

"Maynard, did Mama know you were coming?" Moma asks suspiciously.

"Nope. I know she likes for me to surprise her," he says with a wink. "Where is she anyway?"

"Hmmmp. Out on a date," Moma snorts.

Maynard and Boomer start laughing hard. "Ain't no reason to act like that. One thing about Mama, she's always gonna have a man. Who she out with this week?" Uncle Maynard says, guffawing loudly.

"Oh, you think this mess is funny? How you think she got her arm broken?"

"She slipped on a rock. That's what she said, anyway. That's not the real deal?"

"She slipped on a rock, alright, but she had some help."

Suddenly serious, Uncle Maynard says, "Didn't nobody push her down, did they?"

"No. They just pulled on her until she managed to fall and break her arm."

"Oh. That's better. Lena, let me get that key. I want to be there when she gets in. Did she say how late she was gonna be?"

"Ask Del." Moma nods in my direction.

"Del?" Uncle Maynard turns to me.

"Uh…she said she might be late. I don't know what time for sure, but she and Mr. Smithey were going to dinner and then a play."

"She might be quite late then. That's alright. Me and Boomer can entertain ourselves just fine until she gets back."

"Maynard, you and Boomer know how to act. Don't do nothing *stupid* while you're over there. You and Mary already on bad terms." Aunt Mary caught him riding a young woman in his car a few months ago. Since then, I hear things are a little hairy between them.

"Lena, don't you worry about Mary. I've got it *all* under control. Anyway, me and Boomer just want to stretch our legs and watch some TV. That's *it*," he finishes with a pointed look at my mother.

My mother snorts again. "Del, give him the key. I'll be by to check on her first thing in the morning."

"I'll let her know. See you in the morning. Bye."

"See ya, Lena. Del. Weenie," Boomer says, as he bounds down the steps.

The car cranks up and the sounds of music pounds through the yard again. I can hear laughter as they pull out onto the road. With a squeal of tires, my uncle punches the accelerator and zooms down the road.

"Boy, I can't *wait* until I grow up and can afford a car like that!" Weenie shakes from side to side.

"Why? So you can back it into the *only* tree in the yard, too?" My mother says and walks in the house.

Try as I might, I can't hold back the laughter and I double over hollering.

"It wasn't *that* funny, Del."

That makes me holler even harder.

δ

The night passes slowly. My father returns from work and mumbles incoherent sentences in response to my mother's rantings about Madame A and her going out on a date. It seems like every half-hour she is on the phone checking to see if she had returned home. Uncle Maynard and Boomer must have been having a ball and Moma was interrupting their groove, because the last time she called—around midnight—I could hear her shouting before she slammed the phone down. As I drifted into sleep, I could hear her telling my father that she was going over there bright and early in the morning.

CHAPTER

14

The morning dawns quiet, with only the sound of rain tinkling on the roof. I roll over to savor a few more minutes of sleep before rising. My sleep, however, is interrupted as I hear a bedroom door close sharply and feet stomping up the hall. I stretch and roll out of the bed to find out what's going on.

Moma is pulling on a sweater as I enter the hallway.

"Where're you going, Moma?" I ask, sleep still clinging tightly to my body.

"Over to Mama's. I just talked to Maynard and he says she still isn't home," she replies, shoving her arms into her sweater. "I don't know where she could be. Sick as she's been, she should never have gone out on that date!" She looks hard at me. "Why did you let her go?"

Affronted by her anger so early in the morning, I mumble, "Moma...what could I do? Madame A is a grown woman and—"

Moma turns on me faster than a cornered snake. "Hush! I don't want to hear no mo' stuff about how she's grown. If she was as grown as everybody says, then she should've been home by now. How's she gonna just stay out all night? Y'all just assuming that didn't nothing bad happen. She might be dead in a ditch somewhere!"

"Moma, just calm down. Maybe they had a flat or were running late and decided to stay over someplace."

"Del, my mama's too old to be acting like this! I knew wasn't nothing good gonna come of letting you stay over there with her. You can't handle Mama."

With a shake of her head, she grabs an umbrella and places her hand on the doorknob.

Determined to redeem myself, I ask, "Can I go with you?"

"You better hurry 'cause I ain't waiting but *just* a minute."

I hurriedly throw on the jeans and T-shirt I wore yesterday. Pulling the scarf from my head, I grab a scrunchie and pull my hair into a ponytail. My mother has the car running and I see her shift into gear as I jump over puddles, holding my hand over my head since I didn't get an umbrella. I hop into the passenger side and quickly slam the door. My mother spins gravel as she turns the car and guns it onto the road.

"I don't know *what's* got into that woman! I swear, how hard can it be to pick up the phone and let somebody know she wasn't coming home?"

"Maybe she didn't have a chance or—"

"See, that's what I'm talking about! Y'all *assuming* that ain't nothing wrong. Mama could be *dead!* It's a *good thing* that I decided to keep a close eye on the situation. Shit!"

This is bad. Moma *never* curses in front of us. I remain silent, unable to provide any words of comfort. In fact, my heart was starting to thump loudly in my chest as I imagined a myriad of things that could have gone wrong—Madame A in a bad accident; them getting carjacked or something. My mind swims with scenario after worsening scenario. I clutch the arm of the door and say a silent prayer, hoping that she would be home by the time we arrived.

As we crest the hill, I see only the BMW in the drive. Pulling right on its bumper, my mother hops out of the car before it stops it rocking. Pounding on the door loudly and wiggling the doorknob, she calls out, "Maynard! Boomer! *Goddammit*! Somebody open this *damn* door!"

I hear feet sounding on the floor and suddenly the door is thrown open. "Lena! What the hell is wrong with you?! All this beating on the door and shit ain't called for!" Uncle Maynard yells, his haggard face irate.

"I told you I was coming over. Why didn't you have it unlocked?" Moma yells back just as irate. "Is Mama here yet?"

"No."

"Dammit! Did you call the hospital and check if she had been in a wreck or something?"

"No."

"Well, why didn't you? Do I have to do *everything*? Seems like if you were *concerned*, you would have checked that!"

"When I find a need to be concerned, I will be. Shit, I'll bet Mama and Ol' Smithey are laid up somewhere, not the least bit worried about us. Gal, you acting like she's supposed to report in or something. *She's* the mother, not you. She'll be home when she feels like getting here."

"Mama don't stay out all night! That ain't normal for her!"

"So what? Maybe she decided she was finally old enough to stay out as long as she wanted to."

"I don't care what you say, Maynard, I'm gonna call all the hospitals and see if she is there. If I don't find her, then I'm gonna call the police and file a 'Missing Persons' report."

"Shhhhht. You can't file no 'Missing Persons' report until she's been gone for at least 24 hours. I say just sit tight and go on home. I'll let you know whether she's here by 12 o'clock. If she hasn't shown up by then, *then* we'll figure out what else we need to do."

Moma is not hearing this. "You do whatever you want, but I'm gonna get on this phone and start calling the hospitals now. I couldn't live with myself if my Mama was somewhere laid up in a hospital and we didn't even *try* to find out. Get out of my way." My mother says, elbowing sharply past Uncle Maynard.

I see Uncle Maynard's hands form into fists. He looks like he is ready to strangle her before he notices me standing there, fear written all over my face. His features soften.

"Hey, Del. I didn't notice you with Lena carrying on and such. I'm surprised she dragged you out of bed so early."

"Well, I heard her get up and when she told me she was coming over here, I just hopped in the car. I'm worried about Madame A, Uncle Maynard. You don't think anything bad has happened, do you?"

"Don't you worry none. One thing I know about Mama, she knows how to get out of trouble. I think she's gonna turn up in a little while. I ain't gonna worry until I've *really* got something to worry about."

I nod my head. In the background, I hear my mother on the phone.

"Yes, is this the Emergency Room?"

"No, I need to speak to somebody in Emergency—"

"I don't know anybody that *works* in Emergency, I need to find out if my mother has been brought in—"

"You can help me?"

"Her name's Adoll Bernstein. She's a black female, 75 years old..."

"No, she doesn't have any major medical problems...hold on! She's got a cast on her arm. She broke it a few weeks ago."

"No one? What about a Jane Doe that fits her description?"

"Well, thank you anyway." She finishes and hangs up the phone. With barely a pause, I see her skimming her fingers along the Yellow Pages for another number.

As she begins dialing, I hear a car slowly coming into the driveway. Darting to the door, I feel relief down to my feet as a smiling Madame A and Mr. Smithey roll to a stop.

"Madame A's home!" I shout out loudly.

"Thank goodness!" I hear my mother exclaim in the background.

"I told you she was all right, didn't I? Don't look like nothing happened at all. All that fuss and worry for nothing." Uncle Maynard says.

I step outside, practically jumping up and down with happiness, relieved that all my worrying was for nothing. Madame A was just fine.

"Well, what have we got here?" she says, looking at me standing there when I was supposed to be at home. As my mother and Uncle Maynard walk outside, her face lights up in surprise. "Look what the wind done blown in. Maynard!" Mr. Smithey opens her door and Uncle Maynard rapidly engulfs Madame A in a hug.

"Hey, Mama. I was trying to surprise you by driving down yesterday. How you doing, Mr. Smithey?"

"Fine. It's been a while since I've seen you, Maynard. How are things going in Clinton?"

"Booming. I couldn't wish for it to get any better than it is."

"That's good to hear. Well, it's good seeing you. Hello Lena." My mother just nods her head. "I've got to be running."

Turning back to Madame A, he holds her hand and says, "I enjoyed our date, Adoll. We'll have to do this again."

"We sure do," she replies with a warm smile. "Take care."

"I will. I'll be talking with you a little later."

"Bye now."

"Bye, bye."

Madame A waves as he drives away, a content look on her face. When his car disappears over the hill, she turns slowly. Facing us again, she sighs mightily— one of those "Lawd, Lawd, *Lawd*, what is it now?" type of sighs. Finally, she asks pointedly, "Now, what in the *world* are all of y'all doing here this early in the morning?"

My mother, quivering with pent-up anger not yet expressed, can't wait to talk. "Why you *think*, Mama? You didn't come home or call, so we were worried," my mother responds, anger pinching her face.

"Oh, now I've to tell you when I decide to come and go?" Madame A says, staring at my mother.

Here we go!

"It would be nice. I mean, how are you gonna stay out *all night long* and not say a *word* to anybody? Anything could have happened. We didn't know *where* you were."

"Nothing happened and I told Del that we were going to dinner and a play. Since it was so late when the play finished, we decided to get a room and *relax* for the night." Madame A finishes smugly.

Uncle Maynard is trying to stifle a laugh, his shoulders shaking like a leaf. At this moment, Boomer decides to drag into the kitchen for a drink of water. When Madame A hears the water running, she walks smartly to the door and looks inside.

"Boomer Lett! This Old Home Week and nobody told me?" Madame A chuckles. "I see you spending the night like you did when y'all was younger. You come over here with Maynard?"

Boomer, his chest bare, pants rumbled and barely zipped, rubs the sleep from his eyes. "You might say that." Suddenly he grabs his head, moans pitifully, then says, "You got to excuse me. I've got a serious headache." Without another word, he turns on his heels and walks back down the hallway.

Shaking her head, she looks at Maynard and says, "Let me guess…you and Boomer been in that 'ignant oil' again."

"We had a few beers and stuff, that's all. I'm feeling fine. I guess Boomer can't hold his liquor."

"You know Boomer ain't never been able to hold his liquor. He'll probably be upchucking his guts in a little while. Just make sure you clean up the bathroom after him. Ain't nothing I hate worse that a stinky bathroom."

"Got it." He replies with an OK sign.

"Woooo. I don't know about you folks, but I'm plumb tuckered out. I think I'm gonna go lie down awhile." With that, she turns and walks towards her bedroom. "Oh, Maynard, I ain't gonna find no young gals draped all over my bed, am I?"

"Now you know I wouldn't do anything like that," Uncle Maynard says, trying to appear affronted.

"Now you know you would *try* if I allowed it," Madame A replies and laughs. "Anyhow, I'll talk to y'all later."

"Mama, I was thinking of barbecuing this afternoon since Boomer is in town and all...you think you gonna feel up to that?"

"Maynard, you know I always feel up to a barbecue."

"That's good. Well, you go on and get your rest. I'll wake you in a little while."

"You do that," she says, walking to her bedroom and closing the door.

Uncle Maynard rounds on Moma just as the door closes. "See, Lena, I told you there was nothing to be worried about! Mama *knows* how to take care of herself. You need to start realizing that."

"Shut up, Maynard. I can't believe you're acting like ain't nothing wrong with what she did. You just don't stay out all night with a man at her age. It ain't *right!*" Moma says with emphasis, her finger in Uncle Maynard's face.

"This ain't about her age! You just don't think unmarried folks should *ever* stay out all night."

"That ain't so, but I don't plan to stand here arguing with you all day. I'll see you later. What time is this barbecue supposed to happen?"

"I was thinking we'd get things cranked up around 3 o'clock. Think that will give you enough time to cool down?"

"I ain't hot," Moma snaps. "We'll be here. Come on, Del." Without another word or a backwards glance, Moma walks through the door.

"Del, try to get your Moma's blood pressure down before she comes back over here. I don't want her to pop a vessel and have it on my conscience."

"I'll try, Uncle Maynard."

"Well, you better go on before Lena leaves you here."

"Yeah, she'll do that too. See ya."

"Bye. Don't forget, 3 o'clock."

I nod my head in the affirmative and rush towards the now moving car.

CHAPTER

15

The time plods along as I do imaginary household chores drummed up by my mother. After Weenie and I finish mopping the living room and dusting all the bric-a-bracs lined on the shelves, I find that it is nearly 1 o'clock. Determined to get out of any more housework, I drag my tired body into the kitchen where my mother is preparing dinner.

"Moma, if it's all right with you, I'd like to go over to Madame A's to see if there is anything I can help Uncle Maynard with," I say wearily.

"You and Weenie finished the living room?" she asks, not stopping the brisk stirring of the mashed potatoes to look up as she speaks.

"Yes ma'am. We've swept and mopped and dusted everything. You could eat off the floor in there if you wanted to."

"Well I don't want to, but I'll keep it in mind if I decide to do that. You get your things together and go on over. I'll be there around 2:30. Tell Maynard I'm bringing potato salad and some iced tea. I guess he's probably already gotten the meat, but if he doesn't, just give me a call and I'll bring some with me."

"I will."

Hurriedly, I rush to take a shower and change out of my grungy clothes. Just as I'm tying my shoes, Weenie walks into my room.

"Can I ride over with you? Moma said she didn't need me, so it would be okay."

"Sure. You ready now?"

"Let me grab a sweatshirt and we can ride."

"Good deal."

Grabbing my change of clothes, we quickly load into my car.

δ

Conversation is sparse as we ride over to Madame A's. Driving into the yard, I can see the smoke curling into the air from the patio area. We jog around the rear of the house and see Uncle Maynard and Boomer sitting around a grill loaded down with meat, bottles of bear in their hands. *Guess Boomer's hangover must be over.* Seeing us, Uncle Maynard places his bottle of beer behind the hot tub and rises to meet us.

"Glad y'all came over early." Looking behind us, he asks, "Your mama didn't come with you, did she?"

"No. She said she would be here around 2:30 or so. She's bringing potato salad, but she said to call if you didn't have enough meat to cook."

"We've got plenty. We killed Mama's chickens this morning." Uncle Maynard says with a straight face.

"What?!" I say shocked, looking back over to the chicken coop.

"Just kidding. Me and Boomer went to the store early and stocked up on everything," Uncle Maynard says, laughing at my stricken face.

"Oh. Where's Madame A?" I ask, looking towards the kitchen.

"She's still sleeping. I plan to wake her around 2 o'clock. That should give her plenty of time to get into the spirit of things before we get started."

"What do you need for us to do?" Weenie asks.

"Can y'all give me a hand in the kitchen? I kind of messed it up getting the meat together for the grill. I really would appreciate if you guys could put the groceries up, wash the dishes and wipe down the countertops."

"He's talking to you, Del. You know I don't do the 'girlie' work." Weenie says laughing.

"No, he's talking to *both* of us. It won't kill you to help me in the kitchen. Besides, you do this kind of work all the time at our house," I say, feeling angry that Weenie was over here fronting like this.

"Lena got you washing dishes and stuff, boy?" Uncle Maynard asks.

"Yes, she does, Uncle Maynard," I interject, before Weenie could lie. "He does all that stuff at home and more."

"Shut up, Del, I can talk for myself," Weenie grouses, scrunching his face up in irritation.

"You mean lie, don't you? Don't act like you don't do no dishes 'cause you know you do!" I say huffily.

"Guys. Guys," Uncle Maynard says, his hands held up in front of him. "No need to fight about it. Weenie help Del then come on back out here with the menfolk."

"Aw, Unc. Del ought to be able to do that by herself," he says pleadingly, looking for any escape.

"She could, but it sure would make things go faster if you helped her out."

"That's right. Why should I do everything by myself when you could help me?" I ask Weenie pointedly.

Staring at me like he wanted to make a move, Weenie finally shakes his head. "Come on, Del. Let's just get this over with."

I brush up against him, boiling for a fight, as I walk into the kitchen. Plastic bags line the cabinets and the area around the sink is wet with meat juice and water. Dishes are piled in the sink and pushed to the side on the cabinets. Spices fleck the countertops. I begin opening the bags and placing things inside the cabinets. After a few moments, I notice that Weenie is just standing there looking, not lifting a finger towards any of the bags.

"What's wrong with your hands? Grab a bag and get to unpacking."

"Del, you just like Moma—always trying to tell somebody what to do."

"I'm not. Uncle Maynard told us what he wants us to do and you're standing there letting me do everything. You're gonna eat just like I'm gonna eat so get to helping me."

"You make me sick. If I knew you were gonna act like this, I would've stayed and come over with Moma."

"You act like things were gonna be different at the house. Moma wasn't gonna let you just lie around until it was time to come over here. You would be working your fingers to the nub if you had stayed."

"Yeah, but at least it would be Moma telling me what to do, not you."

A door opens and I hear feet walking up the hallway. Madame A, dressed and looks refreshed from her sleep, stops at the threshold of the kitchen and surveys the area.

Smiling at us, she says, "Now what you two arguing about?"

Irritated with Weenie, I reply, "Weenie says doesn't want to do the 'girlie' work and help me straighten up the kitchen like Uncle Maynard asked."

Her eyebrows raise. "Ain't no such a thing as 'girlie' work. We're all gonna be eating so we all should pitch in where we are needed. What's wrong with that, young man?"

"Aw, Madame A, I get tired of doing things like washing dishes and putting up groceries. It don't seem right for men to be doing that kind of work when there's women around." Weenie crosses his arms.

"A male chauvinist, I see. Well, since you not a 'man' yet, you just help out until you reach that status."

"But—"

"Ah! I don't want to hear another word. Help Del out 'cause you're gonna be eating your share and mine when it comes time to dig into the food."

"Ump!" Weenie huffs and turns his back towards the food.

"Did you want to say something? 'Cause I don't know where you *think* you are, but I ain't too old to handle up on this broom and give you a little 'home correction'," Madame A says, her brows fierce, lips pursed.

"I didn't want to say nothing," Weenie replies lamely.

I just smile as she walks past us out onto the patio.

"Grab that bag over there and put the—"

"I know where everything goes! You just do whatever you're doing and I'll do what I'm doing! I don't need nobody always giving me directions!"

Smugly, I smile at his irritation. I wanted to tell him how glad I was that Madame A put him in his place, but I held my tongue. Lazy conversation drifts to us from the patio.

"Boomer, you've already got a hangover and you're still drinking?" I hear Madame A ask.

"Mama, a beer will knock the edge off of a hangover," Uncle Maynard says.

"Seems like that's what caused it in the first place."

"That's why it's good for the hangover. You know, fight fire with fire." Logical. Just like a lawyer.

"If you say so. It's your head, Boomer."

"I'm feeling fine, Ms. Doll, just fine," Boomer responds.

"That's good. June coming over?"

"She said she might stop through. She's watching the grandbabies right now, so she might have to wait until Sandy gets off work." Sandy is Boomer's baby sister.

"Sandra still up at the fish plant?"

"Yep. She works the 7 to 3:30 shift. Since her and Henry split, Mama's been watching the kids and all. Sandy can't really afford a baby-sitter for all of them right now."

"I remember June telling me something about watching the kids. Saundra heard from Henry lately?"

"I think so. Sandy did mention that he gets the kids every other weekend, so she has a break then."

"I'm sorry things didn't work out, but I'm glad he's acting like he's a daddy."

"Henry wasn't never one to shirk his duties," Boomer nods.

"I know. I just hate that he got into gambling like that."

"It's a shame. Sandy tried to work with him, but after he didn't bring no money home for two months, wasn't nothing she could do but let him go."

"I second that. I wish they had that Gambler's Anonymous around here."

"I do too. It might have made the difference."

"Nope. You gotta want to change," Uncle Maynard pipes in. "GA can't help you unless you want to help yourself. I don't see how anyone can have kids at home and not bring home money to feed them for no gambling. Then I see those jokers come into the office all the time, trying to jump on any kind of liability suit, hoping it will be their 'big ticket,' after they've spent all their money at the casino. Ain't no 'big ticket' out there for most folks. You've got to go to work and save your money to get ahead. Gambling ain't it! I tell you, when they start suing the casinos, they're gonna flood the office for sure."

"And you gonna sue the casinos for them," Madame A laughs.

"Yep. That's my job. I don't have to *like* the client to sue somebody."

"And there's more to life than money."

"Sure is, but money helps the world turn just a little…bit…sweeter." Uncle Maynard finishes.

"Maynard, I do believe you a hypocrite," Boomer says.

"Might be, but I'm a good, *rich* one," Uncle Maynard replies and they all break up into laughter.

People slowly drift in for the barbecue. Moma arrives at 2:30 on the dot with the potato salad and a busload of attitude. She complained so much about how they were cooking the food, they let her take over the grill.

Aunt Brenda pulls up on her heels with Carla, Laquinsa and the kids in tow. Carla and Laquinsa don't even *offer* to do anything. They just sit down, stare and whisper to each other while the kids run amuck around the patio. Madame A finally says something sharply to Carla that I can't hear, but Carla gets up and fixes plates of food for the kids and they quiet down.

Miz June arrives around 4 o'clock, opaque knee-highs showing past the hem of her best Sunday-go-to-meeting dress, limping on her cane.

"June! Glad you could make it." Madame A rushes over and hugs her.

"I'm glad too. Sandy had just made it in the door and I got me a ride over here lickety split! Oh. I got a little surprise for you," Miz June says, her lips pulled back, showing all of her ill-fitting dentures.

"What you got for me?" Madame A says with her good hand on her chest.

"Just wait a minute. He should be coming around the corner any second."

As she finishes the sentence, a tall, dapperly-dressed older man sporting a goatee walks onto the patio. He smiles as he sees Madame A.

"Land sakes alive! If it ain't Cooter Bud in the flesh!" Madame A yells, a wide grin on her face.

"It's me, Doll. You got a hug for an old friend?" Mr. Cooter says, a sly grin on his face. "I see you still looking fine as ever."

"You quit that now." Madame A swats a Mr. Cooter's chest before hugging him just a little *too* long.

Oh goodness. This is one of Madame A's old flames. I hope Mr. Fred and Mr. Smithey didn't hear about this barbecue.

"June, where in the world did you find Cooter?"

"He was up visiting his daughter and when I ran into him in town, I asked him if he wanted to come out here and see you. I know y'all was sweet on each other one time," Miz June finishes conspiratorially.

"Hush up. It's good to see you, Cooter. Grab a plate and find a seat. I want to know what you been up to since I last saw you."

Mr. Cooter saunters over to the food table, stopping on the way to speak to everyone. He grabs a plate and piles it to the corners with food. I don't know how he manages to stay so slim if he eats like that all the time. Madame A joins him and everyone relaxes as they eat and rehash memories.

Then, Mr. Combs shows up with Ray Ray in tow. *Talk about old flames. They're coming out of the woodwork!* Weenie winks as I watch Ray Ray walk towards me, his jeans hugging him in all the right places. My hands feel suddenly sweaty and I hastily put my plate of food down before he reaches me. Ray Ray's nose is now crooked and there are scars on his face. Not too bad looking, but…different from what I remember.

He pulls me into a fierce hug. I see Carla and Laquinsa whispering out of the corner of my eyes. I ignore them and focus on Ray Ray. Ummm. This feels just like I remember.

"Del! Girl, it's been a while," he says, spittle flying from his lips in his exuberance.

"Yeah. Nearly two years."

"Girl, you looking great! I see college life agrees with you."

"You look good too, Ray Ray." And he did.

"Naw. Since I had that wreck…did anybody tell you about the wreck last year?…I know I don't look the same. I tell you I had a *time*. I ain't never been in that much pain before in my *life*!" Ray Ray says, the memory bringing fresh pain to his eyes.

"Well, you still look pretty good to me," I say, trying to shore up his seemingly flagging self-esteem.

"That's good to hear. So, you got a boyfriend up at school?" He looks at me with hope in his eyes.

"Something like that." I see the hope vanish.

"He sure is a lucky fellow."

"I think so, too." *And I'm gonna make sure he knows it just as soon as I get back to campus.*

"You ever think about me, Del?" he asks wistfully.

Here we go again! "Well...Ray Ray, you know we split up on bad terms."

"I'm real sorry about that. I was just young and stupid. I wish I could turn back the time...try to do things right."

"We can't go backwards, only forwards. We can be friends, if nothing else." No need to offer any encouragement when I wasn't interested anymore.

"I guess that's a start."

"Yeah."

Our conversation is interrupted when Mr. Cooter swings Madame A into his arms for a dance. As Jr. Walker sings 'Shotgun,' they jerk and prance about like they are teenagers. Mr. Cooter just manages to duck as Madame A swings around, her casted arm barely missing his face. The crowd hoots and claps, egging them on.

When Madame A shimmies to the floor and back up, I see Moma pinching her lips, her frown digging a ditch in her face.

We are so into the dancing that nobody hears the car pull up and the new guest arrive. Suddenly a loud voice booms out, "Doll! Whatchu' think you doing?!"

Everybody stops and turns to the voice, which unsurprisingly, belongs to Mr. Fred.

Oh, no. Please don't let him act up. Please. Please. Please!

"Cooter, you get on away from Doll! Doll, why you got him dancing all on you like that?!" Mr. Fred shouts, anger dramatically changing his normally easy-going face.

"Fred. What a pleasant surprise," Madame A says, calmly ignoring his agitated state of mind.

"Doll, you heard me! What you doing dancing with Cooter?"

My eyes are round as I watch Mr. Fred tromp through the guests and stop in front of Madame A. Carla and Laquinsa push on people's backs trying to get a good view. I see Uncle Maynard walking closer, a serious look on his face. He stops just behind Madame A.

"How you doing, Fred? It's been a long time since I've seen you," Mr. Cooter says, his hand outstretched like they were meeting amicably. Mr. Fred ignores the hand; stares from Madame A to Mr. Cooter. Mr. Cooter finally drops his hand but steps closer and slightly in front of Madame A.

Madame A shifts back in front of Mr. Cooter. "Fred, now you gonna have to act like you got some sense or you need to go home," Madame A continues on easily.

"That's right, Fred. We're having a good time, so you can either join in or take it to the house. Don't matter much to me either way." Uncle Maynard says quietly, but his eyes are screaming "fight"!

Mr. Fred doesn't take his eyes from Madame A. "Doll, how many men you gonna run around with? Bad enough you got me and Smithey, but *Cooter*? You trying to turn into a—"

"Don't say it! You better not *say* what I think you were gonna say, Fred, 'cause if you do, Miz Easter ain't gonna *know* you when I'm through with you!" Uncle Maynard interjects harshly, his fingers punctuating his every word.

"That's right. Who you think you're talking to, boy?" Mr. Cooter gets his jib in while taking a step forward.

"I got your boy. You get on away from Doll, you old snake," Mr. Fred sneers, as he pushes Mr. Cooter backwards.

Oh! They fixing to get to fighting!

"Fellas!" Madame A yells out as she elbows between them, barely having room since the guest have crowded close around them. "I got this, Cooter, Maynard," Madame A says, patting their chests. "Now Fred, you come over here making a *spectacle* of yourself for nothing. I can dance with Cooter if I want to. I ain't seen him in years and we go *way* back. Back before you was barely out of training pants. I ain't complained about Bertha calling over here looking for you like y'all still living together, now have I?"

I see Carla and Laquinsa 'high fiving' each other to the side. "You tell him, Grandmama!" One of them yells out. *Just like them. They love keeping up "mess."*

"Mama! Bertha's been calling over here about Fred?!" My mother jumps into the conversation. "I knew you dating was a bad idea." Moma looks at Fred meanly. "Fred, you and Bertha still seeing each other?"

"This ain't got nothing to do with Bertha! And so what if I am? Doll seeing every man in the country she want to...so what if I am?" Mr. Fred puffs out his chest with this statement.

"And you're right too, Fred. I ain't married to you and you ain't married to me. We can see anybody that wants to see us, you know that. Bertha *definitely* wants to see you. Maybe you should go and see what she calling up here about."

"But—" Mr. Fred begins, apparently not expecting this type of statement from Madame A.

He better ask somebody!

"Nothing. You just turn around and go on home. You done put my business and yours in the street and you know I don't operate like that! Somebody give him a plate so he can get on out of here!" Madame A says, fury finally exploding out of her.

You tell him, Madame A. My grandmother doesn't just talk the talk, she walks the walk!

"But, Doll..." Mr. Fred says again, just now realizing that he was all but ass out with Madame A.

"I don't want to hear another word! Don't you even *think* about dialing my number again, acting like this. This is *my* house! You're a *guest*! I thought we were better than this!"

"Doll, I'm sorry. Can I please have another...chance?" Mr. Fred begs, uncaring how "low" he was bringing himself. *Can't he see all these folks here?*

"Go on home, Fred."

"Doll, baby, I'm sorry. I just get so crazy in the head when I see other men up around you and all—" Mr. Fred touches her good arm. I see Moma and Uncle

Maynard watching closely, Uncle Maynard ready to jump at *any* provocation, imagined or not. "—and Cooter, I'm sorry for what I said. Y'all go on and dance. I'll just sit over here and not say a word." Mr. Fred finishes lamely, looking for a chair to sit in.

"Nope. You take your behind home, Fred. I'll talk to you when I talk to you," Madame A states with finality, turning her back on him and taking Mr. Cooter's arm.

"Doll—" Mr. Fred pleads, his butt halfway to the seat of the chair.

"You best leave now, Fred," Uncle Maynard interrupts, barely civil.

"But, Maynard, this is a just a little misunderstanding and all—"

"Might be, but Mama says you need to leave, so you gots to go." Uncle Maynard holds his hand outwards towards the driveway. "Thank you, Carla," he says, as Carla places a foil-covered plate in his hands. "Here's your plate, so let me help you to your car."

"But I can fix this…little misunderstanding, Maynard."

Uncle Maynard places a hand on Mr. Fred's arm and pulls him towards the driveway. "Why don't you give it a rest and come on back with some candy and flowers and try again another day?" Uncle Maynard suggests, not pausing in his stride.

"You think?...Why you pulling me so? I can walk...All this 'cause I love your mama. She knows how I feel about her and all..." his voice drops off as they round the corner of the house.

Everyone shuffles back to their cooling plates, but I can feel that the good spirit has left with Mr. Fred. Sure enough, Mr. Combs makes his excuse and walks over to get Ray Ray. I can see that Ray Ray doesn't want to leave, but he does, promising that he would stop by before I left for school. I don't know if that's a good thing or a bad thing. Afterall, I've still got Stefan.

I hear Weenie talking to Carla and Laquinsa, hopping up and down, punctuating the air with wild arm movements.

"Now you think you're a player, Carla, but you ain't *never* gonna be able to handle a man like Madame A!" Weenie shouts with glee.

"That's what *you* think. Boy, you're still wet behind the ears. I know how to handle the men, that's why they're after me like I'm air." Carla gives us a slow wink.

"Yeah, but you don't know how to pick the *good* ones. You just running around with anybody telling you what you want to hear. You ain't trying to find somebody for the long haul."

"Whatchu' mean? Just 'cause I ain't with nobody for a long time, don't mean I ain't trying!" Carla's eyes flash with anger.

"Name one man, one supposedly *good* man, you've been seeing," Weenie insists. I see the cogs churning in Carla's gelled up head. "I'm waitingggg," Weenie pushes her. "See, that's what I mean. You've got the *men,* but ain't a one of them good enough to name to nobody."

"Shut up, Weenie, I can't *stand* your ass anyway," Carla retorts nastily.

"What do you know about women and men anyway? You ain't had no pudding since pudding had you!" Laquinsa chimes in with her negative two cents.

"Might not, but all you've got to do is watch. And I see *plenty* just watching you two 'na-nas' hooking up with every low-down, broke man in town."

"My men ain't broke! They give me plenty of money! You don't even know what'chu talking about," Carla screeches, neck popping with attitude.

"If they're giving you so much money, why're you still up in your mama's house?" Madame A interjects suddenly from behind us. "Seems like since you're so 'flush,' you could pay me back the money I just gave Brenda for y'all's food and stuff."

Carla rolls her eyes but doesn't say a word. Madame A harumps and walks over to speak with my mother.

"Get on away from me, Weenie, before I slap the *shit* out of you!" Carla whispers fiercely as Madame A gets out of earshot.

"I'm going. I'm going. But before I do, you think about what I said," Weenie says with a wink before walking back over to the table and piling another plate up with food.

Aunt Brenda apparently heard some of the exchange because she grabs her purse and tells them to come on. They mumble under their breaths as they take their time gathering up the children and getting two more plates of food *each* to take home. Well, at least the kids will eat something tonight.

I saunter over to Weenie at the table. "That was bad, boy."

"Sho' was, but how many more last names she gonna have for them kids?" Weenie says with a laugh. "Madame A is the real deal. She's got men she dealt with years ago still sniffing up behind her. And when her main squeeze shows up...Del, did you see that?"

"Yeah, I saw."

"When I'm ready to get married, I'm gonna find me a woman just like Madame A."

"Somebody with lots of boyfriends?" I ask jokingly.

"Naw, that ain't what I meant. I meant somebody who won't let me just walk all over them and do anything or say anything I want. I believe I could work with somebody like that."

"That's what you're looking for now?"

"Now? Naw, I'm just trying to understand the game and get my 'hunting' skills down pat. This is my time to play. Right now, I'm just checking out the girls that want to holler at me. *Later*, I'll look for a woman like Madame A. *Later.*" Weenie places emphasis on later, like it will explain his actions now.

"Uh hum. Oho, here comes Moma." I say as I watch my mother bearing down on us.

"Weenie, you ready to go?" Moma asks.

"Not really. I was thinking I could come back over with Del."

"That all right with you, Del?" She looks at me.

"Well...I'm staying. I brought my clothes and everything." *I don't want to go home!*

"I just talked to Maynard. He's staying tonight and I believe Mama has had all the excitement she needs for today. You and Weenie go and straighten up the

219

kitchen and cover the food, then just come on home. Try to be there by nine," my mother finishes and walks back over where Uncle Maynard and Boomer are sitting without waiting for us to respond.

I'm speechless as I contemplate how many chores my mother will find for us between tonight and tomorrow morning.

"Guess you and me gonna be worked to death tonight. Moma is *definitely* in her 'Mommy Dearest' mood tonight." Weenie says with dread.

"Yeah. It's just after seven, so let's just hang loose and put up the food later."

"Yeah."

My mother takes her leave soon after. Madame A, Miz June and Mr. Cooter are giggling as Mr. Cooter recounts tale after tale of his travels all over the country. He left Yokel years ago and got a job with the railroad out of St. Louis. He finally retired ten years ago, but he still travels a lot.

Boomer and Uncle Maynard have their own party going on with some of their classmates that stopped by. Can after can of beer is pitched into the trash, the tink of each one loud in the air.

I finally stretch my legs and begin straightening up the food in the kitchen. Weenie sees me in the kitchen but stays over with Uncle Mayard. It's best. I don't really need his kind of headache right now.

As I wipe down counters, I replay the ugly scene in my mind over and over. Who would have thought that Mr. Fred would have acted like that? He didn't seem like that kind. Goes to show you, there's some caveman in even the nicest ones. Madame A sure showed him, though. I was proud of how she handled everything calmly. She wasn't no 'drama queen,' showing out just for the show. She said what she had to say and that was that. Now, if I—

BBRRRIIIINNNGGGGG!!!!

The ringing phone breaks my revelry.

"Hello?"

"Del, you and Weenie hadn't left yet?" My mother asks hurriedly.

I glance at the clock. It is only eight-thirty. "Moma, you said to be home by nine, didn't you?"

"Yes, but it's dark and I worry about you driving on the road. Mr. Felton's cows were out when I went by, so I want you all to come on home and take your time driving slow."

"Right now?" I ask.

"Yes, right now. What're y'all still doing anyway?"

"Nothing really. Some folks are still here, but I was just cleaning up the kitchen."

"Well, when you finish, you get Weenie and y'all come on home."

"Yes ma'am."

"Bye."

I don't even try to get mad. Wouldn't do me a bit of good anyway. Either I was coming home like she asked or she would be up in here to get us and I *surely* didn't want that. I finish wiping the counters, wrap up a plate of food and go outside to get Weenie. Stopping briefly to tell Madame A we were leaving, I grab a protesting Weenie and walk to the car. Weenie finally shuts up when we get into the car. Driving at 35 mph, the five-minute drive takes fifteen, but we avoid the cows still milling in the road near Mr. Felton's house.

Surprisingly, Moma doesn't ask us to do anything when we get home. I listen to some CDs and watch television with my father. Weenie plays on his Gameboy, Playstation or whatever you call it, and we all climb into bed around eleven.

Chapter

16

Saturday morning.

I stretch lazily and stare out the windows from where I'm lying in bed. Another sunny day to round out my vacation, and *what* a vacation it has been. This week has been a *trip*! Who knew that Spring Break at home in little, old, backwoods Yokel, MS would have this much action? Madame A and her boyfriends…man, if I can learn to handle up on the boys like that, they wouldn't know what to do with me! I giggle to myself as I imagine me acting like her.

I slowly rise and dress quietly, hoping to get over the Madame A's before Moma's good mood broke. Stepping into the kitchen, I already see that I might be too late. Both my mother and father have already risen and eaten, leftover plates of breakfast in front of them.

"Good morning," I chime out cheerfully.

"Morning," my father replies, a smile on his lips. My mother looks at me but doesn't say anything. *Guess I didn't beat the good-to-bad mood break.*

"You're up early, Daddy. Got to plant some more?"

"No. We got everything in the ground earlier this week. Me and your Moma were just talking about the big barbecue Miss Doll had yesterday. I hate to say it, but it's good thing that I work late sometimes." He chuckles with that statement.

"It wasn't *that* bad. We just had a little action, that's all." I chuckle with him.

"That's what Lee was saying. So, Fred finally showed his tail. I knew it was only a matter of time. When he was living with Bertha, one of the reasons they had so many arguments and stuff was 'cause Fred was so jealous."

"How'd you know what Fred and Bertha had going on, Andy?" my mother says bristling, the furrow back in her forehead. I guess she's wondering if Daddy and Bertha have been having conversations she didn't know anything about.

"Oh, Lee, in a town this small, you hear stuff." My Dad shakes his head. "I've been knowing Fred for years and I've seen how he acts around his girlfriends. Why do you think his wife left?"

"I thought it was because they just didn't get along," she says plainly, her hackles lowering slightly.

"Because Fred was so jealous. That woman could hardly get to the store and come back late, or what *he thought* was late anyhow, without Fred driving around town asking everybody and their moma if they had seen her. She must have gotten sick and tired of it, so one day when he was at work, she took off."

"Well maybe she was late and he was just concerned. Ain't nothing wrong with checking up on your spouse if you're married. Things happen to folks all the time." Moma tosses her head before sipping her coffee.

"But fifteen minutes late? That's a little over the head there."

"How do know she wasn't out there sneaking around? She might have been late trying to talk to a man or something," Moma replies, eyebrow hitched.

Just like her to say something like that.

"I don't. But I do know that grown folks don't like being treated like children. That woman could come and go just the same as you and me. Being married don't give nobody ownership of your body, you know that," my father asserts.

"You might be right, but folks don't leave 'cause somebody checking up on them *unless* they've got something to hide, Moma says in her best Miss Prissy imitation.

"Folks leave for any little reason now. It don't take much and they're out the door." Daddy wiggles his index finger at her.

"So, Mr. Fred has always been jealous?" I interject, trying to stop an argument about folks that don't even live here.

"Yep. Every since I've known him, and that's been thirty-five years or better. He ain't acting no different than he always has. Y'all just ain't never seen that side of him, but it's there alright."

"You can say that again."

My mother remains silent. Knowing that any moment she would find a chore for me to do, I hastily ask, "If it's all right, I'd like to go on over to Madame A's house."

Moma glances at the clock. "Why do you need to go so early? It's only a little after eight. They're probably still sleeping."

BBRRRIIINNNGGG.

"Wonder who that is this time of morning? Hello?" My mother asks, concern lacing her voice. "Yes, Mama, she is up—"

Hallelujah! God strikes again!

"Hold on." She holds out the phone for me. "It's Mama."

"Hello." I say, trying to cover up my happiness with some dread in my voice. I was hoping Madame A wasn't gonna have something else to do that would keep me here any longer than necessary.

"Hey Del, I'm glad you already up. I know your Moma is sitting there staring up in your mouth right now." Sure enough, my mother was watching my every sentence.

"Yes, ma'am."

"Well tell her I want you to come on over here right now. I know she's just about to get into one of her fits about what happened over here yesterday, so tell her I need you to come over right away. Maynard is leaving soon, so tell her that."

"Moma....Madame A needs me to come over *right* now."

"What? Something happened after I left last night?" I see the alarm in her face.

"No. Uncle Maynard is getting ready to go, so she needs me to come over and help straighten up things," I improvise. I was hoping that Madame A was listening in case Moma got back on the phone.

"Well...that's fine then. Go on. We're not planning to do anything today anyway."

"Madame A? Moma says that's fine. I'm coming right over." I hang up before she can speak another word.

Grabbing my sweater from the coat rack, I fairly run out the door and hop into my car. As I gun the engine and prepare to back up, I see my mother walk out on the porch, arms flapping .

What now?

I slowly roll down the window, expecting another delay from her. "Del, call me if Fred comes back over there starting some mess," she yells out to me.

"I will," I reply hurriedly and begin rolling backwards.

δ

Reaching Madame A's house, I see Uncle Maynard's car is still in the same spot. I park and walk in the front door. Madame A is sitting at the table reading a newspaper, a cup of tea by her elbow. The only other sound is the television tuned to CNN.

"I thought Uncle Maynard was leaving," I say as I sit down besides Madame A.

"Oh, that was just something I made up to get you out the house. Maynard's back there sleeping like a baby. As much as him and his friends drunk, he might not get up until after noon."

"Boomer still here?"

"Naw. Boomer left with June and Cooter."

"That's good. So, what're we gonna do today?" I ask, hoping she wasn't planning to send me back home.

"Well, chile....me and Cooter gonna go and see a movie. Samuel L. Jackson's got that new one out and ...ummm *ump*, that Sam Jackson sho' something to look at! If I was just forty years younger, he wouldn't know *who* LaTanya was."

I burst out laughing. My grandmother hooked on *Samuel L. Jackson*?

"He doesn't know *what* he's missing." I assure her. "What about Mr. Fred and Mr. Smithey? None of them coming over, are they?"

Her face clouds up. "Fred don't need to say shhhht to me and Smithey is out of town visiting his daughter up in Batesville. I've got nothing else to do, so me and Cooter gonna go out and catch up on old times."

I thought that's what they were doing last night!

"Ah...Madame A, you and Mr. Cooter used to date too, right?"

"Yep, right after I found out about Raymond. After Raymond...girl, I was in hurt-a-man mode. I was gonna punish somebody's son and Cooter somehow ended up volunteering. Whatever I dished out, Cooter worked with me. Never said a *word*, even when I was mean. We had a time! Me and Cooter wasn't in love or nothing, but he was somebody alright to pass the time with."

"How long has he been gone?"

"Oh, Cooter's been gone from 'round here more than forty years. He got that job up on the railroad and he ain't been back since."

"Was he...*married* when y'all were dating?" I ask this tongue in cheek. She could slap the mess out of me if she thought I was being too forward.

"Who, Cooter? Cooter ain't never been married! Least not that I ever knowed! Chile, Cooter is what the Temptations call a 'rolling stone.' Wherever he laid his *hat* was his *home!* And he apparently laid his hats around a lot of homes, 'cause he's got six children all up and down the Mississippi."

"Dang! And he wasn't married to any of the women?"

"Not a single one. I guess he was like the young fellas nowadays...keeping his options open." She winks.

"So, what did you see in him?"

"Cooter was something good to look at, girl! You can't tell it now that he's gotten older, but that Cooter cut a sharp blade when he was younger."

I can't see that at all.

"Yeah, Cooter took me all out and about and we had us a good time. Then, when the train job came through, he was gone and it was over." Madame A snaps her finger.

"Just like that? Y'all didn't try to get together and keep things going?"

"Wasn't nothing to keep going. Cooter and me was just having fun, nothing serious. So when the job came through, I was happy for him and wished him the best. You can't hold on to folks trying to make them stay around just for you. Let them go. Besides, there's millions of men in the world. If one ain't available, you can bet another is!"

"You're a trip, Madame A!" I say with admiration. Madame A acts like a *man*. "Ah, I been wanting to ask you...how in the *world* did you marry a Jewish man?"

"Bernie...old Bernie." Her eyes take on a wistful look. "Bernie was the first man that treated me like Edgar did. Manners...did that man have some good manner! When I walked into that restaurant and he pulled out my chair...I couldn't believe it! There I was in Baton Rouge, LA, and a white, *Jewish* man is pulling out a chair for a colored woman? Girl, you could have bought me for a plug nickel."

"What's so good about that?"

"This was a few years after the Civil Rights demonstrations and stuff. We had just gotten into their hotel and restaurants pretty regularly, but the folks still acted all funny with us and all. Not Bernie, though. He treated me just like any other customer, white or black. I noticed him staring at me while I ate, so I kept going to the ladies' room to make sure I didn't have food on my face or lipstick smeared around my lips. He probably thought I had the runs or something." She laughs loud when she says this. "When the meal was finished, he said the entire thing was on him! Then he asked me for a date! Del, I was scared out of my mind. I was in Baton Rouge, eating at this restaurant trying to show my cousins that I *could* eat in it and here this white man is talking and acting like I wasn't colored."

"I can see how that much have scared you a little." Shucks, when I go in a restaurant now that doesn't have a lot of Black people in it, I feel a little scared. Of what? I don't know. The people don't really act strangely, but I think it's just something *in* all Black people. A radar or something. They may not say anything "politically incorrect," but we just *know* they don't want us there anyway.

"A little? A lot. But something about how he acted let me know that he wasn't trying to set me up to rape and lynch me with a pack of his buddies. I felt my stomach clenching with excitement while he kept on talking so, I said yes."

"And that was it?"

"Oh, no. We dated a while before we got hitched. We went on our first date that night I met him, though. He took me on a carriage ride through these beautiful gardens and talked to me about his life. I told him a little about mine, but not much. He was widowed and had two daughter living up in Minneapolis. He had left Minneapolis 'cause he was tired of the cold and the snow. He wanted someplace warm for his later years."

"So he moved all the way down to Baton Rouge?"

"Yep, and opened up a restaurant. It was a nice establishment too—crystal and china on the table, the waiters in black with bow ties, bowing and nodding without attitude. He must have had to train them for a while to get them to act like that."

"He sure must have," I reply, thinking how it takes an act of Congress to get any type of decent service in a restaurant today.

"We got to seeing each other nearly every weekend. Me going down there or him up here. He didn't really like coming up here 'cause the folks treated him something awful—calling him names and pointing at us—so we got together down there. And boy did he like to do the town—theater, plays, opera. Then one day, he tells me he wants to marry me. Me! I was having fun and

I wasn't really thinking about no marriage, but he wanted to get married to me bad."

"Were you scared?" I ask excitedly.

"I was *real* nervous about marrying a white man," she says, shaking her head, her hand held in front of her face. "I know, I had dated my share with Smithey and Thumper, but didn't nobody *know* about them. If we got married, then the *world* would know. I mean, we were going to go out in public all the time as man and wife. Maynard and Brenda hadn't said much about him, but your Mama...chile, your Mama was something different."

"But you married him."

"Yes I did. And it was one of the best things I *ever* did. He wasn't no Edgar, but he was a strong second."

"What did his daughters say?"

"Why, nothing much to me, anyway. I wasn't expecting them to call me Mama, just treat me with the respect you would give your father's new wife and they did, calling and checking on us and visiting regularly. I was at the christening three of his grandbabies and nobody even blinked."

"Wow. Minneapolis sounds like a color-blind place."

"In patches, only in some patches. They've got the same types of folks everywhere—good, bad, bigot—they still in every city and town you travel. You've got to remember that."

"I will."

"Me and Bernie had us a fine life. We lived in a big old gingerbread-looking house downtown. Girl, I liked to have hollered when he told me we were getting a maid. A maid! Usually somebody was trying to make me the maid, not work for me *as* a maid."

I laugh at how delirious she must have felt. If my husband wanted me to have a maid, I'd be delirious too.

"Yes, indeedy, we had a good life in the gingerbread house."

"I don't remember that house. Did we ever visit you?"

"Nope. Your mama wasn't too keen on me dating, much less *marrying* a white man, so she never really came to visit. I usually saw y'all whenever I came home."

"I was little, but I remember when he died though. It was in his sleep, wasn't it?"

Madame A's face takes on a sad, faraway look, "Yep, right in his sleep. We had been married for 15 years and he dies in his sleep. Your mama brought y'all up for the funeral, but she turned right around afterwards and came on home. Didn't stop by the house or nothing."

"She was still upset after fifteen years?" *Moma definitely needs to learn to let some stuff go.*

"Your moma knows how to hold a grudge. Of course, I don't know why she had a grudge in the first place, but you know how your moma is."

"Yeah."

"After Bernie died, I got a quick offer on the restaurant and sold it to the first person that came up with the cash. Me and his daughters split the million-dollar life insurance policy he had and I sold the house for a pretty penny. Then, I came back here, since life down there had lost its sparkle for me, and built this little palace of mine," she says, spreading her arms wide.

"And pissing Moma off some more."

"And did I piss her off! Girl, I thought I was gonna have to take a shovel to her head when I told her what I was gonna put out here!"

"A shovel! Oh, she just didn't want you to stand out real loud. You know Moma don't like nobody calling attention to themselves." *Unless it's her, of course.*

"What's wrong with standing out? I like being different, that's why I built what I wanted. I saw a house like this down in Brazil. I always said that if the Lord let me get a piece of money, I was gonna build me one just like it. Bernie's death gave me the money, so I hopped on it."

"And you been making the folks' tongues wag around here every since."

"You know they've always been wagging, but so what? Every last one of them knows that if they had the choice, they would be living right up in here with me."

"You're right too." *This house is the* bomb!

"I know it! I had so many folks just 'dropping by' after I finished it, I thought I was gonna have to charge admission. You'd of thought we were at the circus or something!"

"Quit!"

"Would too. Even Easter's dry behind came slinking up in this place and you know me and her been on the outs for years," she says, rolling her neck like Miz Easter had committed a grave sin and should have known better.

"Why is that, anyway? I'm sick of hearing the gossip, so what's the real deal?"

"Some fool notion Easter got in her head that me and Slim—that was her husband—was fooling around."

"Were you?" *She has traveled that road before, you know.*

"No. He was asking, but I wasn't taking him up on no offers. When Easter caught us talking besides the church one Sunday morning, she tried to say I was coming on to him. But the truth was, *he* was coming on to *me*," she huffs with plenty of attitude. "She was acting so silly that I didn't try to clear things up and Slim didn't either. He just let her go on thinking that I was up to no good. That let me know *right there* that he was just a no-good sucker out there trying to get his Johnson wet. A typical man—hen-pecked and scared to death of his wife—trying to see whose skirt he could lift on the side for fun. Just weak, and girl, you know I ain't got *no place* in my heart or on my body for no weak man." She looks disgusted.

"She's been mad all these years and you hadn't tried to get it all cleared up?" I mean why take the blame all these years? They might be missing out on a good friendship.

"That's right. Slim been dead going on ten years and she's still mad. When I was up at the cemetery for Memorial Day visiting Edgar's grave, I stopped and read Slim's tombstone since they only recently got one. Anyway, she comes tromping her old tail across that grass and asked me why I stopped at Slim's grave. I just looked at her and walked on. She must think I'm gonna dig him up and jump on his dead, shriveled up pecker! With all the live ones out here? I ain't spending a minute pining after no dead one, that is, not unless it's Edgar. The man's dead and she needs to get over it, plain and simple. As crazy as she still acts, I'm kinda mad I *didn't* have a go at him. He must've had *something* to work with in those pants of his." Madame A gives me a shy nod.

"Must have if she's still mad at you!" I scream out.

"She needs to thank God it's too late for me to find out now!" Madame A hoots and we both giggle.

"Seems like nearly every argument people get into is about either sex or money."

"Yep. That about sums it up. Sex and money. The things we do to *get* and *keep* both of them ought to get us a First Class seat to Hell. We'll kill, steal, lie, cheat and conspire against our own children for either one of them. Yeah, sex and money are the root of all evil. I know men say women are, but that's a lie. It's really sex and money and the hold it has over us."

"They seem to be pretty powerful, that's for sure. All the girls at school talk about is who's driving what expensive car and how the guys need to give them money or they aren't gonna deal with them. Humph. Like the cars they're driving didn't come from their parents' money. Don't nobody hook up for love anymore, it's all about the money."

"And don't forget about the sex. Like I told you earlier, women have been acting a fool about men's Johnsons for years. All this huffing and fighting for six inches. Shoot, I saw some stuff in a magazine, some *battery-operated* stuff you can buy, that would put a man's member to shame."

"You're reading sex magazines, Madame A?!" I blurt out with astonishment. Every day Madame A surprises me just a little bit more.

"Yeah, why not? I'm old enough to and besides, I like to be well-*rounded* in worldly things."

"I'll bet," I say unconvinced. The one and only time I snuck and looked in 'Playgirl', I wasn't trying to keep up on current events. "You looked at the pictures too, didn't you?"

"Not really. You see one, you've just about seen them all. A magazine don't take the place of the 'real' thing, it just shows you your options."

"That's what y'all calling it today? Options?" Uncle Maynard voice booms up the hall from the bathroom. "Mama, you're acting like a female pervert! What kind of mother looks at men's naked pictures in magazines?" He walks to the kitchen, a deep frown on his face.

He had no business eavesdropping anyway.

"A live one. Y'all looking at every naked picture that comes by your face. Don't really need to buy no magazines today with all the girls just about naked when they come out the house. How many times *you* put your hands over your eyes or looked away?"

"I figure that they ain't got no clothes on, they must want me to see, so I look just like every other man in America."

"And China too. How come it's alright for men but not for women? What's good to the rooster, good to the ginny!" Madame A cackles.

"Yeah, Uncle Maynard. Why is that?" Time to get an answer to this question, straight from a man's mouth.

Uncle Maynard looks from Madame A to me then throws his arms in the air. "Ain't y'all got something else you need to be doing besides talking about men's privates? Y'all don't know *nothing* about men. You're just guessing."

"What do you mean *I* don't know nothing about men? I raised you without your daddy, didn't I? I know what men, young and old, talking about, thinking about and trying to do about what they talking and thinking." Madame A slaps her hands on the table for emphasis.

"Yeah, Mama." Uncle Maynard nods a placating nod, an "I feel ya" nod. You know, the type boys always give girls when they don't really want to hear what we are saying but act like they do, and begins walking back down the hall.

Madame A bristles. "I know *plenty* about men! Shit, wasn't for women, wouldn't be no men. Women been molding, building up and tearing down men for millions of years. We already knew the game before y'all even begin *playing* it! We might not say nothing, but ain't no mystery to no *men*. Y'all read like an open book. All y'all really interested in is sex—"

"—and *money!*" I chime in, completing the sentence.

Uncle Maynard slams the bathroom door hard. *You think we got under his skin?* In the silence afterwards, Madame A resumes sipping her tea and reading her paper as I watch CNN.

"Uh, what time y'all going to the movie?" I ask, finally tired of the daily dose of world horror on the news.

"Oh, he should be here around noon. We're going to the matinee at one o'clock."

"Y'all don't need no company, do you?" I ask. If Moma found out I was staying here alone while Madame A was out, she might find something else for me to do back home.

"You want to go?"

"Yeah. I like Samuel L. Jackson, too. You think Mr. Cooter will mind?"

"Naw. You might just enjoy talking to ol' Cooter. We gonna to eat at Pearl's afterwards."

"If you think he won't mind, I'd really love to go."

She waves my doubts away. "It will be fine. What? You think me and Cooter gonna want to make out or something?"

Like she's not still making out.

"No. I didn't know if you wanted me to hear y'all catching up on old times."

"We caught up pretty good last night. To be honest, I just want to get out of the house and do something. After Fred acted a fool last night, I'm tense and I don't want to be cooped up in here."

I look down at my well-worn jeans and sweater. "Can I wear what I've got on?"

"Sure. You look fine. Besides, I'm the one ought to be getting gussied up for Cooter, not you."

"You're right! The *last* thing I want is for Mr. Cooter to think I'm trying to catch *his* eye." I say playfully.

"Girl, don't say that unless you been a passenger on Cooter's train *at least* once." Madame A responds with a knowing smile.

"I'll pass." The image that begins forming in my brain goes mercifully black.

CHAPTER

17

The movie was over way too soon for me. Samuel L. Jackson showed *out*! Madame A oohed and sighed so much, I thought she was having an attack of something. When she wasn't ogling Samuel, she and Mr. Cooter acted like they were my age—holding hands on the sly and I even saw him trying to cop a feel on Madame A's knees. She popped his hand pretty loudly and he stopped after that. *I guess she doesn't want another ride on the Cooter train either.*

Riding over to Ms. Pearl's place, I am finally able to ask Mr. Cooter about his travels.

"So, Mr. Cooter, Yokel any different than when you left?"

"Not really. You've got some of the same folks still walking the streets, just a little older. I see the General Store has been replaced by Bill's Dollar Store and there's more doctors' offices and stuff, but basically the atmosphere is still the same."

"You sorry you didn't move back down here?"

"Nope. Yokel is a little slow for my blood now. After living in places with plenty of action, I just don't see myself coming back and slowing way down to play country gentleman. I would go crazy."

"Don't you have a daughter here? Why not move closer to your family?"

"I've got family in St. Louis, Memphis, Helena, Greenville and Vicksburg, and all them places are better suited to me than Yokel."

"But...it's home," I say. Everybody wants to come home, don't they? I mean you can work all over the world, but in the end, you just want to get back to where you came from. Be with people that have known you since before you became whatever you ended up becoming.

"Well, I always believed home was what you made of it. It ain't where you come from, it's what you do where you are. I could move down to Yokel and be miserable, so I ain't really home, or I could stay where I am, with all the friends I've made over the years, be happy *and* feel at home. Home just mean different things to different folks. Besides, our old home place was a rented sharecroppers shack that's probably been bulldozed by now."

"Yep. They put in a new housing complex over where y'all use to stay nearly ten years ago. That old shack was one of the first things to go. Of course, wasn't nothing to it no more, just a raggedy lean-to." Madame A affirms.

"See what I mean? I ain't really got no *home* here no more."

"So what is St. Louis like?"

"Real nice, real nice. We've got plenty of industry, good schools and with the casinos, work can be had by anybody looking for it."

"Sounds like a good place."

"I think so."

"How long are you gonna be down?"

"I don't know. I'm enjoying myself and renewing some *old* friendships, so I'm just gonna go with the flow, as you young folks say."

I chuckle with that statement. "You gonna visit any of your other children?"

"Yes. I've seen one of my sons already, so on my way back, I'm gonna stop off at all the others and stay a little while with each of them."

"I hear that you've never been married. How did you manage that?"

"Miss Del, marriage is for some people, it just ain't for me. I don't want nobody keeping tabs on me and telling me what I ought to be doing or what I'm not doing for them. I gotta be free to be me. I let 'em know up front what I'm offering and not a drop more. You know," he says, cutting his eyes at Madame A, "if we give y'all an inch, you'll take the whole damn mile and a half."

"Who you talking 'bout, Cooter?" Madame A feigns anger.

"Nobody you know, Doll. You and me always had an understanding and we ain't never changed the agreement that I know of."

"And I'm gonna keep it like that. We're friends. Period. Nothing more, nothing less," Madame A says, flustered.

"Calm down, Doll. That's what I was saying. What I tell you I'm gonna give you is *all* I'm gonna give you. Nothing more, nothing less."

"Alright, then. You need to be glad I wasn't serious about us 'cause if I *was,* I'd a had you strung out like a Christmas turkey. I would've made you cook yourself then jump up on the platter so we could eat you." Madame A's head cocks with this pronouncement.

I burst out laughing. Madame A talking smack at her age!

"Oh, you would, would you? You know…it ain't too late for you to see if you still got them kinda of skills. I've got a Viagra pill in my pocket. Thirty minutes then…*watch out*, Mama!" Mr. Cooter eyes twinkling.

"Oh, yes, it's too late. Your heart wouldn't be able to handle me now."

"It handled you just fine forty years ago, so since you and me both the same forty years older, I figure I can keep up with you. Why don't you try it?"

"Nope. I don't want your daughter crying and yelling over to my house 'bout how I killed her daddy." Madame A smiles, fanning at her face with her good hand.

"We ain't gonna worry about her. When she sees the smile on my face up at the funeral home, she's gonna know I went out just like I wanted to. And just think, you're the one put me there. Talk about a testimonial! 'Stuff good enough to kill!' Folks will be running you down, Doll, running you down." He guffaws at this.

"They're already running her down. That's how she broke her arm!" I say, throwing in my three cents.

"Hush up, Del, don't be putting my business in the street!"

"I'm sorry," I say without a bit of remorse.

"I ain't surprised. I knew when Fred acted up at the house, you still had the men acting a fool about you. Miss Del, when I was living 'round here, nearly every man I knew wanted to sport Doll on his arm."

"Really?" This was a dishy tidbit here.

"Yep. She was high-class, though. Couldn't just anybody step to her. You had to be about something, going somewhere, or she didn't have *spit* for ya."

"Ain't nothing wrong with that, Cooter. A woman needs to have high standards 'cause if she don't, y'all will just use us up and dump us off without any thought in your big old heads."

"Now, that ain't how it is," Mr. Cooter begins, shaking his head. "Sometimes, women read more things into the package than what's on the label. There's plenty of women that start out with a no-good man and think they can change him. That's the wrong kind of thinking. Y'all need to realize, what you start with is just about what you gonna finish with. Men don't really change unless they've got a reason to change. But if it ain't in them...it just ain't in them. You need to start with something good, to end up with something good."

"Boy, those are some words to live by there!" I say.

"Uh hum. Women always attracted to the 'bad boys.' They ain't been good to nobody else, so why y'all thinking they're gonna do you any different? And when they don't, y'all cussing and fussing them 'cause you frustrated you couldn't change them. Just don't make no sense to me. Misery makes you old and you can see from my young face, I ain't let no misery live 'round me!" Mr. Cooter continues.

"You will if I bust you up sides the head with my cast!" Madame inserts with glee.

We all laugh at that remark as we park in front of Bugles and Banjo's. Ms. Pearl is no where in sight when we enter and the hostess seats us.

"Where's Pearl today?" Madame A asks the hostess.

"She's in the back. Do you need to see her?" I see fear on her face when she asks this. I guess she thinks Madame A has a complaint against her already.

"Yes. Please ask her to come out here."

"Yes ma'am," she says as she seats us in a booth.

Ms. Pearl ambles towards us within a few minutes. Today, she has her hair wrapped in a bright yellow turban and is sporting a deep purple African dress.

"Doll! Two times in one week! Girl, either my cooking is getting better or you're just starving."

"Pearl quit. I just wanted you to see who I ran into." Madame A waves her casted arm towards Mr. Cooter.

"Who is this? Your face is familiar... but, I don't know..."

"It's Cooter Bud, Pearl! You remember when me and Cooter was an item, don't you?"

"Cooter! That you!" Ms. Pearl says and pushes all of her onto Mr. Cooter for a hug. "I hadn't seen you since Mary had Baby Jesus."

"Pearl, it's me alright. How you been?"

"Fine. Just fine. How long you staying? Where're you staying?"

"I don't know how long, but I'm up at my girl's house."

"How she doing? I haven't seen her in years."

"She's fine. Doll tells me that this is your place."

"Yep. All mine. Doll helped me get started and I've managed to make a go of it."

"I see. How are the kids?"

"They're doing fine. All of them moved away except Miner, you know my son that's got some problems."

"I remember."

"Well, they're all doing good. They come down regularly and check up on me. I'm proud of all of them."

"Excuse *me*," Madame A interjects looking from Mr. Cooter to Ms. Pearl, "Pearl what you got good today? I'm hungry as a two dogs, so could we order then catch up on old times?"

"Don't worry, I ain't trying to drive on your territory, I'm just happy to see Cooter. We've got the same things we've always got—greens, chitterlings, hog maws, pig's feet, barbecue, seafood—"

"What the special?" Madame A interrupts.

"Pork chops with rice and gravy, collards, corn bread and blackberry pie."

"Good Lawd! Y'all know how to make a man want to move back home! I haven't had no blackberry pie in years!" Mr. Cooter says with excitement lacing his voice.

"It's good, too. Y'all just want the special?" She looks around at each of us.

"Del? You think that's okay or do you want some of them *nasty* oysters again?" Madame A asks, her nose wrinkled up in distaste.

"No. The pork chops sound good." I say, not wanting to have Madame A acting up over the oysters again.

"Give us all the special then. Can you come and eat with us?"

"Why sho'! I know the woman that owns this heah place, so it will be alright." Ms Pearl adds, rolling her eyes.

"And bring some iced tea with you, will you?"

"Yes, Missus. I will, Missus. Anything else you and Masta want?" Ms. Pearl says, bowing and nodding in buffoonery.

"Get on with your foolish self! I've still got that number for the Better Business Bureau in my purse. Don't make me use it," Madame A threatens.

"Don't make them white folks come and whip your behind 'cause you got the best place to eat in town shut down!" she chuckles. "I'll be right back."

Mr. Cooter looks around the restaurant and says, "This is a real nice place. We sho' didn't have no places like this to eat when I lived down here. Times have achanged."

"You remember that juke joint up on Hwy. 28 we use to go to? The one where you had to compete with the flies to eat? Del, they gave us a flyswatter with the meal," Madame A squeals.

"Ugh! A flyswatter?" *How nasty can an eating place be?*

"That was Yo-Yo's, wasn't it?" Mr. Cooter asks.

What kind of name is Yo-Yo's? Sounds like a Chinese food place.

"Yep, that's the one. Del, y'all missed good times eating in little shacks like that. Wasn't much to look at from the outside, or inside either, but they had some gooood food up in there." Madame A sounds like she would really like to be there right now.

"Sure did. The ribs would slap the back of your brain, they were so good."

With flies buzzing around? Uh uh.

"And later on, the place would be packed with folks trying to get out and ease their minds from a day of work."

"Yeah. We packed into those places like lice on a hog. Wall to wall women and men. They got to fighting nearly every night. Boy, those were the days." Mr. Cooter smiles widely.

I'm glad I missed them. "Well, we don't go to juke joints, but we go to clubs and they get to fighting there pretty regularly too. Seems like a club can't stay open longer than a year or two before they shut it down, usually after somebody kills somebody or cuts them up good," I explain.

"Uh hum. Yo-Yo had a big old double-barrel shotgun he kept under the bar. When the folks started getting out of hand, he would just shoot off a round into the air and they would clear out. I'll bet he had to put new tin on the roof every time it rained. He didn't try to stop nothing outside, just on the inside. Plenty of folks got messed up in Yo-Yo's parking lot. He didn't have no phone, so when something went down, you had to load them into a car and drive them to the colored doctor over in Fayette. A lot of folks died from foolishness," Mr. Cooter says sadly.

"What were they fighting about like that for?"

"What do you think, Del? That old sex and money," Madame A says pointedly.

"If a man *thought* you were looking at his old lady, he would slap the mess out of you. Then…it was *on*! Ain't no man that's a *man*, gonna be slapped by no other man in front of a crowd of people. That's cemetery shit there!"

"Still is. It's one thing to fight about a man that's coming onto your woman and she don't want him too, but it's stupid to fight about a woman already giving it up out of both legs," Madame A says.

"Yeah. Seems like folks got a lot more rage inside them today. The young folks mad about anything and everything, ready to fight at the drop of a hat. A lot of gals egg that mess on. They know what they're doing with these men, so they should be women and handle their business. Don't just stand there and act like you don't know why he's touching on you and you've been letting him!" Mr. Cooter says, shaking his head.

"Now, wait a minute. Men act the same way. Plenty of men will let women fight over them and not lift a *finger* to straighten out the mess. They want their cake and a beer to go with it, too," Madame A tells him off, her index finger speaking with her.

"I say, unless he's disrespecting me, I ain't got—" Mr. Cooter begins.

"See, that's what I mean," Madame A says, cutting him off. "Y'all don't care that he's disrespecting *your woman*, y'all mad 'cause you think he's disrespecting *you*."

"He is. A man can't look like no man in front of his woman, if he allows another man to disrespect him, *in front of his woman*, and say nothing. You just messed up your own playhouse there."

"Y'all always worried about yourself. Don't think about the woman at all, do you?" Madame A stabs Mr. Cooter in the chest with her finger.

"Doll...all I'm saying is, you might can act one way when there's nobody around, but in front of other folks...you got to put up or shut up."

"And women be damned!" Madame A shouts.

"What y'all talking about that got you so stirred up, Doll? I could hear y'all yelling back in the kitchen," Ms. Pearl says, walking quickly up to the table.

"Cooter 'bout done made me mad talking about women and men and how they act." Madame A's lips push out in anger.

"Well, why don't we talk about something else? Y'all 'bout to scare my other customers. You know they're scared of us anyway and when we get to shouting and carrying on, they might run out of here and that just *might* be bad for my business if folks see others running out of here, you know," Ms. Pearl says, sarcasm dripping from her lips.

That makes all of us chuckle and tempers cools. Ms. Pearl slides into the booth after she places glasses and a pitcher of iced tea on the table.

"What's been going on in Yokel since I last saw you, Doll?" Ms. Pearl asks.

"Nothing much." Madame A says and I start to snicker.

"What's so funny? What'd Doll do now?" Ms. Pearl asks, looking at all of us.

"You tell her, Madame A. Tell her about the barbecue," I prompt.

"Barbecue? I didn't know you had a barbecue, Doll. Guess you didn't want me to come," Ms. Pearl pouts.

"Girl, Maynard had a small barbecue since he was in town. He did it all of the sudden. Wasn't nothing planned or I would have invited you. That's where I saw Cooter again."

"Oh. So, what happened?"

"Fred acted a monkey. Showed his behind 'cause me and Cooter were *dancing*. I just got so mad at his ass, I told him to get on back to Bertha."

"Sho' did." Mr. Cooter shakes his head.

"No! Doll, you know Fred is a jealous man. Oh, he looks all nice and quiet on the outside, but you know he's a damn fool. Susanna was right to get away from him."

"I don't care how jealous he is, he ain't got no call to be over at my house acting like he did. I told him to lose my number 'cause I got ain't *shit* for him."

"I know you did. How'd he take that?"

"I don't know. Maynard showed him out and me and Cooter got back to dancing."

"Girl, I don't know what to do with you! First, men tussling over you break your arm, now you almost to start a fight at your own house. What you got in that body of yours? Looks like we need to bottle it up and sell it on the street. I can see it now, 'DOLL'S COOCHIE POTION. GUARANTEED TO MAKE A MAN ACT A FOOL!' We'd be millionaires in a week!" Ms. Pearl's arms are wide like she is holding a marquee.

"Stop it, Pearl." Madame A shakes her casted arm at Ms. Pearl.

"That's what I told her too." Mr. Cooter laughs.

"No, you stop. You've got cocaine in your breath or *something*, the way they acting and—" Ms. Pearl stops suddenly as she stares back at the front of the restaurant. "Oh, look who y'all done talked up!" She whispers, "If it ain't Fred Chaps…and he's with Bertha!"

"Where?" Madame A asks, rising out of the banquette slightly.

"Hold on, Doll, you with me today. You know you got to leave with the man you came with." Mr. Cooter says, placing a hand on her arm.

"I am. I'm just trying to get a better view so I can have all the facts when he comes calling back over to my house." Madame A says, patting his hand.

At this moment, Mr. Fred looks over and sees us. He freezes and Bertha—they ought to call her Big Bertha because she's at *least* 300 lbs. wet—continues on behind the hostess unawares. Mr. Fred's mouth is hanging open, a look of surprise on his face. I didn't know if he's surprised that we caught him out with his no-longer-living-with-him live-in lover while he's begging Madame A every chance he gets or because Madame A is with Mr. Cooter.

Bertha realizes that he's not behind her and when she follows his line of vision, her face becomes pinched and angry. *This is a look she should definitely put in the trash. It doesn't do a thing for her.* She tromps back up the aisle—everything jiggling and jumping—grabs Mr. Fred's hand and pulls him towards their table. He roughly pulls his hand back and follows along. I can see Bertha whispering fiercely to him as they walk to their table.

"Can you believe he didn't even greet us?" Madame A drolls.

"What'd you think he was gonna do? He's over there with Bertha after trying to act jealous at your house last night, how did you think he was gonna act?" Ms. Pearl says.

"I thought he would wave or something. All that talking he's been doing is just a waste of time. A front. Well, Bertha can have him. He don't need to come sniffing 'round my door no more."

I look at Madame A to see if she is only trying to appear brave or if she truly didn't care. From the nonchalant look on her face, I didn't think she really cared one way or the other.

"I guess him seeing me with you didn't help. I'll bet he can hardly eat with the indigestion he just got," Mr. Cooter pipes in.

"You think they will stay and eat? I think Ms. Bertha's gonna leave," I say, hoping that Ms. Bertha didn't come over to our table starting no mess.

"Naw. Fred's gonna wait it out. He wants to know what me and Cooter up to." Madame A says, years of experience in these matters in her voice.

As the food arrives, Ms. Pearl tells us, "Y'all go ahead and eat. I'm gonna greet my new customers. I'll be right back."

Before Ms. Pearl reaches the table, Bertha stands suddenly, upsetting her chair, and stomps towards the front door. Mr. Fred looks over at us...slowly rises and without another look in our direction, follows her. We sit with our mouths open as he walks out the door.

"Dog! I wish we had bet on it! I could have picked up a couple of dollars!" I look at them and exclaim.

"Ain't this something...Fred following behind her like a puppy. Pearl, looks like you need to bottle up Bertha's coochie, not mine," Madame A giggles as Ms. Pearl returns to the table, surprised as the rest of us.

"Sho' something, ain't it? I wouldn't have thought ol' Fred would've done that. Doll, what'd you put in that man's water?" Ms. Pearl looks at Madame A, perplexed.

"Ice."

"Must be some crack mixed in it 'cause he's got it bad. Seems like Bertha knows it or else they would've stayed."

"Bertha might talk a lot of noise on the phone, but she ain't willing to try it in person. She worries about what folks say too much. This way, she can tell the folks she showed me. Made Fred leave and all." Madame A clucks her tongue.

"Yeah, but you and me know, she just showed us how she ain't really got nothing there but hope. And I think she hoping he don't see you again."

"She gonna go home and rock that man's bed for *sho'*! Might even break his back! She's got to reestablish herself 'cause he done showed her how much he cares for you, Doll. What's her number? Maybe I can *console* her some before I leave," Mr. Cooter says impishly.

"Well, that's your best out, that's for sure." Madame A says with a hoot.

"Let's dig in folks. The show is over...for now." Ms. Pearl says and begins eating.

And is it ever!

CHAPTER

18

Mr. Cooter drops us off at the house after we eat. Uncle Maynard's car is gone, so I guess he's already left to go back to Clinton. As we drag our food-laden bodies in the door, I hear Mr. Cooter joking with Madame A.

"What'd you say Bertha's whole name is again? I might need to check up on her for real," Mr. Cooter ribs.

"It's Bertha Harris. From the way things look though, you might need to call Fred Chaps' number. She's probably back up in there."

"Well, I'll try her first and just go from there," Mr. Cooter says and gets back into his car.

"Better you than me. Don't let her smother you 'cause you know that's a *lot* of woman to work with."

"Don't worry about me. I like a woman with some meat on her bones. Them po' women will puncture a lung with them skinny elbows and knees. Besides, she'll keep me warm." Mr. Cooter laughs and winks. "Y'all take care now. Bye."

With a wave, he drives off.

"You think he's really gonna call Ms. Bertha, Madame A?" I ask.

"Probably. He's a man and they ain't known to be choosy when there's a willing female around," Madame A snorts. "Bertha's gonna have his old ass walking with a cane when she gets through with him, though. He'd better ask to stay on top or it's all over for him."

"Poor Mr. Cooter. I sure hope he was joking."

"We'll know when we see him trying to get around with a walker!" Madame A doubles over with laughter.

"You think Mr. Fred's gonna call or come over tonight?"

"He probably stupid enough to, but I plan to blister his ears if he does!" Madame A says indignantly.

"Why do men act so jealous with one woman while they are running around with another? The boys at school are always trying to holler at one girl while they still have a girlfriend. Then they act up real bad when they think she's seeing somebody else and he's doing the same thing. Seems like double standards. It's okay for a man to be on the hunt, even when he has somebody, but it triple wrong when a woman does it," I moan.

"It's a mess, all right. Somehow, men think just 'cause you like them a little and spend time with them, you've got a 'OWNED BY' label tattooed across you ass or something. A jealous man makes life go a whole...lot...slower. He won't let you have any freedom while he has all of his. They don't cut a woman any slack. Let him catch her messing up and see what happens! Men don't give women second chances. You're out the door on your butt. Then they expect us women to forgive them when we catch *them* and they want us to hear all their begging and pleading for forgiveness. We don't want to hear that *shit*!" She shakes her fist.

"The only advice I give is, do what you want to do with whoever you want to do it with. Cooter was right. Tell them up front whether you're looking for something serious or just a fling. That little understanding between a man and a woman will, hopefully, keep down confusion. Ain't nobody got no reason to be jealous if you just lay the cards on the table where they can see them. After that, it's on them," Madame A finishes.

"I don't know any guys that will deal with you if you tell them you don't want anything serious. They'll call you names and before you know it, you'll have a bad reputation," I say, thinking about how guys on the yard have labeled some really nice girls I know.

"Reputations be damned! Men hadn't realized it yet, but we've got categories for them just like they've got for us. We've got the ones we want just for their bodies or the ones that's good just to talk to and the ones we want to take home to meet our mamas. The key is that *you* have got to figure it out and let *him* know early in the game. And if you don't know right off, tell him when you realize he ain't gonna make the 'Home to Meet Mama' cut. Don't let him go on thinking he's The One. That will get them mad and showing out on you." Her index finger drives her sermon home.

"But why are they so jealous in the first place? I mean, women aren't *nearly* as jealous as men."

"Yes they are. They just hide it better. Men, now they've got to brag and boast to their friends about their girl. It's alright when they're talking about her, but don't let another one look at her, nosiree! That's when the old jealous monster starts to rear its' ugly head. The next thing you know, he's watching his girl like a hawk; trying to keep up with her every move. And it's all his fault!" Madame A is working herself up now.

"Why?"

"'Cause he been spouting off his mouth when he should have just stayed quiet! Probably bragged about how good she treats him or what she has or how good she is between the sheets. Just stuff better left unsaid."

"Yeah. Most girls know that if you tell your girlfriends about your man, especially the between the sheets part, you're just advertised for some competition where you're least expecting it."

"Uh hum. But that's how men are. They've always got to be one up on the other fella. Us women are just pawns in the game. A possession to show off."

"That's so pitiful," I whine.

"Might be, but that's sho' how they are. Why, one time—"

BBRRIINNGGG!!!!

"Hold that thought while I get the phone, Madame A," I say, trotting over to get the receiver. "Hello?"

"Miss Del, is Doll there?" The frantic voice of Mr. Fred reaches out to me.

"Ah...yes...hold on." I place my hand over the mouthpiece. *It's Mr. Fred,* I mouth to Madame A.

"What's he want? I told him not to call over here...let me have that phone." Madame A grabs the phone from my hands.

"Yes, Fred?"

"Ah hum...Well, didn't I ask you not to call me no more? Seems like you and Bertha hitting it off good again, so I don't see no need for you to call on me no more..."

"Is that right? You're telling her *something* or else she wouldn't of acted like that—"

"Huh? What're you crying about? Ain't nothing else to be said—"

"I don't want to hear nothing about no Cooter. We're friends, that's all. You need to get on back to Bertha 'cause I ain't interested no more—"

"That might be, but I'm sho' gonna try and find out—"

"Listen Fred, you just got kicked out of Doll's World. You have a good night, now, you hear? Bye." With that she slams the phone down.

"See that mess right there? A jealous man, no, a *weak* and jealous man ain't worth the salt in the soup. I told you he was probably gonna call, didn't I? I know men! Maynard don't know nothing about his old mama. You know what Fred had the nerve to say?"

"You can't find nobody else like him?" I reply, because that's usually what the boys tell us when we leave them.

"Yep. How'd you know? You must be learning something from all my preaching. I'm glad to know I ain't just gabbing my gums for nothing. You're picking up the right information. Just stay a little while longer and I'll have the boys eating off your toes."

"The hands will do just fine." I say, thinking how nasty it must be for somebody to eat off your toes.

"Well, I've got to get my afternoon nap in or I ain't gonna be a bit of good to nobody breathing," Madame A says and walks into the bedroom.

δ

While Madame A naps, I watch television and think and think and think some more. I realize that since I've been home, Stefan hasn't called even once. Well…maybe he called me at home and my mother or Weenie forgot to tell me. I hastily reach for the phone and dial the digits.

"Hello?" My mother's voice sings into the phone.

"Hey, Moma. What'cha doing?"

"Nothing. I'm just folding clothes and cooking dinner. How's your day been?"

"Oh, fine. I went to a movie with Madame A."

"And who else? I know Mama didn't go alone with just you." I hear the peevishness in her voice.

"Ah…Mr. Cooter came with us and we stopped by Ms. Pearl's to eat afterwards."

"I knew it! Fred one day, Smithey the next and now Cooter. I tell you, that woman has got men on the brain! What in the world is she thinking about? I'll bet the folks in town are just wagging their tongues about her. It's like Peyton Place over there!"

"Moma?" I say, trying to stop her tirade, "Did I get any phone calls?" Hopefully, I wait for her answer.

"No…are you expecting a phone call?"

Deflated by her answer, I reply, "Not…really. I was just wondering…since I haven't been there and all." *Why hasn't Stefan called? I gave him my number before we left. How hard can it be to call for just a few minutes and say hello?*

"No, nobody's called for you except Mama."

"Alright."

"What is Mama doing now?"

"She's napping. We ate so much she just came home and fell into the bed."

"Cooter still there?"

"No. He just dropped us off and left."

"Well, thank God for small mercies. You gonna stay over there tonight or come on home?"

"I was going to stay here."

"What about packing? Don't forget you go back to school tomorrow."

"I haven't forgotten. I'll just get everything together in the morning before we go to church."

"Well, if you're sure—"

"I am. That will be plenty of time."

"Alright then. Oh, I smell the cornbread. Let me check on it. I'll talk to you later."

"Bye, Moma."

"Bye."

Hanging up the phone, my feigned happiness deflates. *Stefan hasn't called.* The reality of what this statement means hits me hard. *He's just playing with you; keeping his options open.* Uh uhhh! I know…maybe he was working and couldn't call! I'll call him…*No!* I finally manage to stop the hand reaching for the phone. Madame A was right. He's saying one thing but his actions are shouting out something else. If he really liked me like he said he did, he would have called, *at least once*, to check up on me. He knew Madame A was in the hospital, so you would think he would be concerned. No, I'm not gonna call him. In fact, when I get back to school, I'm gonna start looking at my other *options*, just like him.

The sound of a motor rumbling and backfiring draws me to the window. I see an old Dodge truck with a mint paint job shooting up the road. When it stops, the dust flows around it. A horn sings out loud in the tune of 'Happy Days Are Here Again.' A head leans out of the window and I see that it is Ray Ray. *What in the world is he doing here?*

Slowly, he gets out of the car, wiping the dust from the door with a rag from the back pocket of some well-worn jeans that outline his tight butt. My stomach clenches involuntarily. I grab my midsection, find my legs and walk to the door to greet him. As he rises from wiping the dust, he notices me standing by the door.

"Hey, Del." Ray Ray says, a big smile showing his perfectly white teeth.

"Hey, Ray Ray. What brings you out here?" I feel a multitude of emotions looking at that smile.

"Oh, I was just riding around and I thought I would see how you were doing. You're going on back tomorrow, aren't you?"

I open the door and step outside. "Yeah. After church. You're going back tomorrow too, right?"

"Yep. Spring Break sure goes fast around here."

"You can say that again."

"Oh, I wanted you to see my old truck. This is the one my Daddy had. He gave it to me and I fixed it up and painted it. You remember this old truck, don't you?"

Did I? I remember riding across pastures in search of an isolated spot so we could kiss and feel each other up and dream about our future together. I remember eating sandwiches off the tailgate at the church picnics. I remember confronting him about Yasmin and pushing him off the seat when he admitted he was seeing her! Oh, I remember that truck *too* well!

"Yes, I remember it." I say, clenching my teeth together.

"Looks good, doesn't it?"

"You driving it back to school?"

"Naw. This old thing ain't dependable. It's good to ride around in 'round here, but I wouldn't trust it for long distances."

"Oh. I was kinda wondering about that."

"What you been up to today?"

"Well, I went to a movie with Madame A. We saw Samuel L. Jackson's latest."

"I'll bet you were excited about that. I know you always liked to see Sam Jackson."

"I must say, I enjoyed myself immensely."

"Ah huh. Del...is it alright if we sit down a minute? Del, I just wanted to talk to you again. After I had to leave the other day, I couldn't stop thinking about you and what we might have been."

Here we go surfing down Memory Lane again. "Oh, Ray Ray, that was a long time ago. We were just kids then."

"Maybe, but you were my first love, girl." He grins.

First love? When were we in love?

"I was, was I? I didn't realize that we were in love at all. You sure didn't act like it. In fact, you acted like you didn't even want a girlfriend at all, remember?"

His face contorts in anguish. "I'm sorry about all that. It was just my hormones acting up and Yasmin was telling me all kinds of good stuff…I just wasn't thinking with my head, you know?"

"Oh, you were thinking with your head, it just wasn't the one on your neck!" I set him straight.

"I know, I know. I'm apologizing for all that. I did you wrong, no two ways about it. Plain and simple, I was a low-down, lying, cheating, dirty dog-acting boy."

"Yep." I nod.

"But, I'm a man now. I realize that what I did was boy stuff. It took some time, and a few girls, but I know what I'm looking for now."

"And what's that?"

"A good woman that knows who she is and where she's going."

Well, he certainly doesn't want me, 'cause I don't know diddlysquat. "Who'd you have in mind? Somebody I know?"

"Who do you think? It's you. I miss all the fun times we had. We were just kids the first time around, we're older and wiser now," he says, serious.

"Ray Ray, we're only 18. Yes, we were 15 when we dated, but I don't think we've gotten too much more knowledge since then."

"You might not have, but I sure have. Del, after that accident, I realized that life is meant to be spent happy. All those girls I was running around with? Not a one of them came and visited me or called after the first few weeks. Weeks when I really *needed* some support. And when I got back to school, after they saw me...I might as well have been the invisible man. They weren't interested in having me holler at them anymore. They wanted me for only my looks, not for who I was *inside*. And without those looks...'See ya, don't want to be with ya.'"

"Dog! I didn't realize that things were like that." *That must have been miserable.*

"Well, they were. I'm not mad at them 'cause I might have acted like them too... once. But now...you remember the old saying, 'walk a mile in my shoes?'"

"Yes."

"I've walked that mile and it ain't got no pretty scenery along it. It's rough and ugly. That's how I was— superficial, mean-spirited when it suited me, a user—all those things that folks shouldn't be."

"Now?"

"I enjoy life. I wake up everyday glad 'cause I woke up. I try to do good to others and for others. I know God is working on me and with me each and every minute."

"Ah hum." *Another preacher in the making.*

"Oh, I'm not ready for the pulpit...I can see on your face you're wondering just that...I'm just saying that I realized that I didn't want to be how I was before. I wanted to be somebody that a girl is proud to be with because of the me *inside*, not the outside package."

"That's a good way to be," I speak with real admiration. At least *one* of us has their stuff together.

"I know it...now. I just want you to know it too. I'm not asking for...I don't really know what I'm asking for, but I sure would like it if we could be friends again."

"We can be that."

"And maybe later...we could..." The hopeful expression is back.

"Hold up!" I say, my hands in front of me. "Let's just take the friendship ride for now."

Ray Ray nods, but I can tell it's not what he wanted to hear. "How's your friend up at school treating you? You really like him?"

"I thought I did, but after this week with my grandmother, I've realized that some things I've been accepting just aren't right," I reply quietly.

"Like?" He motions with his hands for me to elaborate.

"I mean...he seems to like me, then I don't hear from him for days. He doesn't like to hold hands and he only comes to see me at night. When I see him out with his friends, he doesn't have much to say to me, like he's always busy and what they are doing is more important than me, you know? Then he tried to change everything about *me*—my hair, my weight, my clothes..." I stop, embarrassed at revealing so much.

"Uh huh."

"Sound pretty messed up, doesn't it?" I wring my hands together.

"Well...I was like that too. It doesn't mean he don't like you, he's just not making you his first priority." Ray Ray hikes an eyebrow.

"What *is* his first priority then?"

"Everything else. You fit in when you're convenient for him. What do you say when he shows up at night after ignoring you in the day?" he questions.

"Nothing. I just go ahead and talk to him," I admit, shamed.

"That's what most girls do and men have gotten use to just doing girls like they want to and they really don't think twice about it. He might like you, but right now, he likes all the other stuff more."

"That's what Madame A said too."

"You need to listen to her. If you would just give me *little* chance, I would show you how a man's suppose to treat his girlfriend." I hear the plea in his voice.

"And how's that?" I ask nonchalantly.

"With respect. No 'in the closet' relationship. I would walk around with you and act like I'm glad to be with you."

"You would, huh? What about your roving eye?" I remind him.

"Shoot, that sucker got plucked out in the accident. It's a good thing I can see at all." We break up in laughter at that.

As the sun drops, we continue sitting on the porch, relaxing and enjoying each other, reminiscing and talking about the future. Not our future, but the future in general. When he finally rises to leave, I hate to say it, but I am truly sorry to see him go.

"I know I've talked your ears off, but I really enjoyed myself. Ray Ray smiles that big, gorgeous smile again.

"Me too."

"Del, is it alright if I call on you when you come home this summer?"

"Sure."

"Give me your number up at school. I want to check up on you and see how things are going."

"Really?" I am surprised at his request.

"Yep. Oh, you still think I'm playing, don't you? Well, I'm not. I gonna work with this friendship thing for now, but sooner or later, we're gonna have to try 'us' again." Ray Ray finishes and opens the truck door.

"We'll see, we'll see." I respond without conviction. The second time around for most couples I know was usually worse than the first time.

"Well, take care now. I'll be hollering at'cha!" He says, his rear end flashing out of my view behind the open door.

"Bye." I wave him down the drive and out onto the road.

Entering the house again, I see Madame A sitting at the table, a smirk on her face.

"I didn't know you were up, Madame A. How long have you been out here?"

"Long enough," she says, still smirking. "That fellow has come a long way, hasn't he?"

"Sure has. I almost didn't recognize the new Ray Ray."

"He's changed, that's for sure. From hellion to heaven bound. That young man has his head on straight. Oh, I know he wasn't always like that, but sounds like he's finally grown up."

"*Way* ahead of me."

"Oh, you're growing just fine. That Combs boy has been through some stuff and tough time will either make you stronger or wimp you out like a jelly fish."

"He's *definitely* stronger." I had to admit that.

"And he'd make some fine great-grandbabies for me," Madame A deadpans, while I look at her like she's gone crazy. "No need to look like that, I ain't got you married off to him...*yet*. I'm just saying that a man like that might be worth the trouble getting to know real well."

"I already know Ray Ray." I protest.

"You knew the *old* Ray Ray. The glimpse you got of the *new and improved* Ray Ray ought to make you sit up taller and take notice. Men that respect you and treat you like a queen are like needles in a haystack—you can't find it until the cow shits it out in the manure and it stabs your feet through your shoe."

"Stop!" I giggle.

"That's right. But when you finally find that needle, you just take a bath and wash that old shit off of you and thread that sucker."

"And then?"

"You sew up that relationship tight and that's that. Can't nobody get out no tight stitches easily. It takes a lot of work, pulling and finally cutting, to do it. A loose stitch can pull out real easy. Snip off one end and out it comes. But a tight stitch...baby, that's the *key*." Madame A emphasizes.

"I think I'm following you, but…I'm not sure." I say, feeling confused as all get out.

"Just let it ruminate a little bit. It'll come to you," Madame A responds, smacking her lips

"I sure hope so."

"I do too."

"You going to church tomorrow?"

"Why sure."

"What time do you want me to pick you up?"

"Don't you worry about me. Cooter's gonna give me a ride. He said he wanted to go to another service in the old church before he left this place."

"You sure?"

"Positive." Madame affirms with a nod of her head. Rising, she stretches and looks back at me. "I don't know about you, but I'm gonna watch some pay-per-view tonight. They suppose to have a *wrassling* showdown between The Rock and Steve Austin. That ought to be something with both them muscular men flipping each other 'round the ring. You do whatever you want, but if anybody calls, just tell them I'm—"

"—in*disposed.*" I finish and laugh with her.

CHAPTER

19

We stay up so late watching the wrestling, I manage to oversleep Sunday morning. Madame A rouses me when she rises so I can go home to pack. After she refuses my request to cook breakfast, I hurriedly dress and ride over to our house. As I walk in, I see that my mother is partially dressed in her slip, stockings and a bathrobe.

"Hey, Del," she sings out happily. My mother is always happy on Sunday mornings for some reason. Must be the Holy Ghost invading her body once a week.

"Hey, Moma."

"You're getting in a little late. You'd better get a move on if you plan to get all your stuff loaded into the car before Sunday school."

Sunday school? I haven't been to Sunday school since the last time I was home.

"Ah, Moma? Is it alright if I miss it this morning? I really need to get everything together so I can leave right after church," I ask, a plea in my voice.

"Miss *Sunday School*?" Moma says, shocked horror on her face.

It's not a sin, you know.

"You know we always go to Sunday school around here. I don't know what you do up at school, but you know you're going to Sunday School and church when you get home. So you might as well throw your stuff in some bags and stuff them in the car, 'cause you're *going* to Sunday School, missy!" Moma finishes, her hands on her hips, happiness nowhere evident on her face or body.

The Holy Ghost has left the building!

"Aw...I'm already late and I barely have time to get dressed and get my stuff together," I whine.

"Why're you so late, anyway? Y'all stay up late with one of Mama's boyfriends?"

"No. I just couldn't get to sleep last night, so I guess I forgot or something." I didn't add *why* I couldn't sleep, which was, of course, Stefan.

"Well, you almost grown so you need to learn to take the lumps when things don't go like you hoped. Suck it up, get dressed and let's go to church."

"But—"

"Ah! Get dressed, Del," Moma says in her sternest voice.

"Yes ma'am," I say, trudging down the hallway towards my room.

As I pass Weenie's door and speak, I see that he is shining his shoes, a tie and freshly pressed shirt beside him on the bed. My father is doing the same as I walk pass their room. Quickly, I throw things haphazard into my suitcase and backpack. Calling Weenie, he helps me to get everything into the car and I jump into the shower. Exiting the shower, I realize that I've packed my shoes for church. After much cajoling and pleading, Weenie finally agrees to go to the car for my shoe bag. As I slip my feet into my shoes, my mother calls out, "Let's gooooo!" I lead the way in my car with them following behind.

δ

The churchyard has a few cars in it as we drive up. I see Miz June pulling herself slowing up the steps and some children running down the other side of the steps. As we enter the church, I quickly find a seat and grab a Bible from the back of a pew. Turning to the chapter for the lesson, I try to focus, but find that I drift off after a few moments while from the droning of the elderly teacher's voice. A sharp jab wakes me and I look into the harsh face of my mother. I sit straighter and try to focus on the lesson, but I drift in and out again after a few minutes. Thankfully, the lessons ends and I reach into my purse for collection money. Placing a dollar in the plate, I eagerly await the dismissal.

The people walk around and mingle a few minutes with the new arrivals before the Church service begins. Ray Ray enters with his family and I go to greet his mother and father. Madame A and Mr. Cooter arrive and people exclaim loudly as they greet Mr. Cooter again. As I find a seat near the back away from my parents, Ray Ray sits next to me.

At eleven o'clock on the dot, "Sweets" begins playing and the choir marches down the aisle and into the choir stand, their flowing robes billowing as they keep time to the beat. Madame A winks as she passes and I wink back. The choir sings heavenly and the people jump up and down on that new song they had been having problems with at practice. Finally, Reverend Blackjack steps to the pulpit, his "entourage" trying to blend in with the deacons and choir members, but still we know it. I stare at him as he begins his prayer.

Reverend Blackjack has what folks call "good hair"—curly and black as midnight. His profile and light color makes me think he must have some Indian or white ancestry in his blood. Thick across the chest and in his robes, he cuts an imposing figure. I must say, he looks like *somebody's* savior up there extolling the word.

Reverend Blackjack's wife, Mrs. Barbara Blackjack, sits on the front pew, a study of "First Ladyism," wearing her tall hat, sequined suit and matching sequined shoes. With every pause in prayer, she lets out a loud "Ah-*man!*" Another woman, sitting in the second row, seems to be competing with her in praise as she also loudly yells out "Hall-le-lu-*yah!*" with every pause. I wonder to myself if she is Reverend Blackjack's new "churchgirl of the month." As Reverend Blackjack's praying gets fiercer, I see Mrs. Blackjack stand, eyes closed tight; hands lifted toward the heavens, loudly repeating "Ah-*man!*" Her potential competition also rises and sways as she repeats her "Hall-le-lu-*yah!*" I giggle to myself at the foolishness of it all. *Did the one with the loudest praises get to be with him tonight or something?* Thankfully, Reverend Blackjack ends his prayer—that I haven't heard a word of—and they both sit down.

As the sermon begins, the door to the rear opens. I turn with the rest of the "nosy" congregation to see who is coming in. Mr. Fred stumbles in the door and the ushers guide him to an available seat near the front. Madame A scrunches up her face and rolls her eyes when he nods to her.

Reverend Blackjack continues his sermon "Stop Getting Your Earlybird Reservation to Hell." He boldly speaks against adulterers, fornicators, liars, homosexuals, gossipers and hypocrites. You'd think that would alienate nearly everybody here, but the church rings with "Say it!" "Tell it again, Rev!" and "Don't hold your tongue! Preach!" As many women as he's been running around with, I couldn't believe he had the nerve to talk about anyone else's sins.

Finally, he ends his sermon and asks all sinners to come to the altar to confess their sins and find the Lord. Now, there should have been a stampede to the front, but the only soul that comes forward is...Mr. Fred. I see Madame A hang her head and shake it as he sits in the Sinner's chair. The Church Secretary whispers with Mr. Fred then she looks to the congregation and indicates that he would like to confess his sins and ask for prayer. Reverend Blackjack asks Mr. Fred what he wanted to confess.

Mr. Fred turns to the congregation. "Ah...I know y'all already know me and I just felt like...I had to come and get something off of my chest." He pauses and looks up at the ceiling. "I haven't been living my life like I was supposed to in God's eyes, well, I don't think any of y'all have, to be honest, but this ain't about y'all. I want to confess and ask all of y'all's forgiveness 'cause I've been a fornicator..." A loud gasp is heard from some of the deaconesses, "...and I've been envious and jealous. You see, I met a really good woman, a woman I really care about, and yes, we've been sleeping together..."

Good gracious me!

"... and running 'round town like we're teenagers and I've been acting pretty jealous lately." I see Madame A shoots poison darts from her eyes into Mr. Fred's back.

"But you see, I know I ain't right. I know I ain't been doing right by being with her like we have been."

You can say that again

"I just came up here to say to her, you ain't got to worry no more. I'm gonna stay away from you until I think I can come to you like I'm supposed to. Like a follower of Christ would. We ain't gonna be laying up no more..." I see my mother looking at him meanly, my father's hand on her arm as if he were restraining her. *If he says my grandmother's name, I don't know what Moma will do!*

"...I'm just gonna get myself together and *then* we'll just see. We'll see. So....Bertha, you free of me......"

Bertha?!

"...You go on and live your life and I won't interfere with yours again. Thank you." With that, Mr. Fred sits back down. A loud wailing begins over in the new annex part. I can't see who is crying, but I'll bet it is Bertha.

The church is quiet as we let all this information sink it. Reverend Blackjack looks flushed and confused. Flustered, he calls for the collection and sits down without a blessing for the sinner or a "rebuke the devil" speech. The collection plates moves along the pews and the choir sings a rousing song, I guess to return the Spirit to the building, 'cause it sure flew the coop with Mr. Fred's speech. The benediction is swift and in short order, I find myself outside standing with Ray Ray.

"You leaving right away, Del?" He asks, holding my hands lightly in his.

"We're eating at Ryan's then I'm hitting the road."

"Well, I hope you will think about what I said. I'm gonna be calling you to help you remember, in case you forget."

"I won't."

"Oh, shoot. I see my mother waving at me. Let me get on over there with my folks. You take care of yourself, now."

"I will."

With a brief, tight hug Ray Ray walks towards his folks. Madame A rounds the corner of the church with Mr. Fred in hot pursuit.

"Fred, leave me alone! You just confessed what a sinner you are, so why you want to start sinning again so soon?" Madame A has her good hand held up, palm outwards, towards Mr. Fred's face.

"That was *Bertha* I was confessing about. You and me got a *heavenly* relationship. I can feel it! Just give me another chance, Doll! That's all I'm asking, just another chance!" Mr. Fred says, walking sideways as he tries to talk into Madame A's face.

"Fred, I see Del and she's got to go on back to school so I'm gonna have to talk to you later."

"But, Doll...what about us?"

"There is no *us*? What part did you miss?"

"But..."

"Bye."

Madame A walks with purpose over to where I'm standing. Before she reaches me, I see Bertha run from the church, tear tracks still on her face, and over to Mr. Fred. She pulls on his arms and says something he must've not wanted to hear 'cause he shakes her off before stomping to his truck. He spits gravel all over the place as he pulls out. Bertha stands there, her face crumpled and devastated. Her sorrow flows in waves over to me and I can't help but feel compassion for her pain.

"Mr. Fred is a mess," I say, shaking my head.

"'Sho is. He just got up there and gave a 'selective' confession. He confessed only the part he wanted to, not the whole thing.."

"I'm glad he didn't say your name."

"He is *too*!" Madame A says with attitude. "I'm sorry I wasted any time on him. Now that he's publicly gotten rid of Bertha, he's gonna worry the stew out of me."

"Why can't he go on? He acts like you put the roots on him."

"Baby, it wasn't no roots, it was my mojo."

"Mojo?"

"Yeah, my mystique; a woman's black magic. If a woman knows who she is and what she's working with, that old mojo is a powerful thing. It's way worse than roots, it more like a drug. Once you're addicted, it's hard to get rehabbed. Fred's just in the early stages of withdrawal and he's just trying to get a 'hit' of me."

"Shoot, I need some of that."

"You've already got it. It's in all women." Madame A grows serious. "Baby, I know you been having some problems with your boyfriend up at school. Yes, I heard what you and Ray Ray were talking about...but let me tell you something...ain't no man got the *right* to treat you disrespectfully. You make them act right or kick their butts to the *curb*! I know you're unsure about a lot of things—your looks, your weight, what you wear—but you've always got to remember, don't settle for anything to just say you have somebody. Just because it's warm and walking, don't mean it ain't dead weight. You set the standards and the pace. If he can't tow *your* line, cut that sucker loose. Don't be who you *ain't* 'cause eventually who you *are* is gonna catch up with you."

"This up and down elevator ride of relationships…it's just all confusing. I don't know what to do or what to say. I feel like I'm just drifting along sometimes."

"I'm not gonna tell you I ever felt like that 'cause I hadn't. I found Edgar early on and he was my standard. I couldn't accept less than that. I know you think you hadn't found anybody like what I told you your granddaddy was like, but I think you have. You're just looking for it in the wrong body. Sometimes you don't have go pass your own yard to dig up a treasure. Now your young man up at school probably got some redeeming characteristics, and if you also think he's worth the trouble, work with him. But if you don't, cut him loose and make yourself available for a true blessing. A real diamond. You know they come dirty and rough before they get cut and polished, but when you do get them cut and polished…you just can't *help* but to show it off to the world! And that's what I'm hoping you will do.

Keep your options open, 'cause you've said more in what you haven't said than in what you have."

"It's that obvious?"

"Only to a woman that's been around the block a few lifetimes."

"Oh, Madame A, I don't know what I...this whole week...it's was what I've been needing—a life lesson that I didn't have to live through to get. If only I had talked with you before...I could have saved myself a lot of stress and worrying about stuff. Instead, I could have been happy being who I was and saying what I wanted and acting like I needed to. One thing I do know, me and Stefan gonna have to start all over. You think he'll do that?"

"If he don't, you'll be all right anyway."

"Yeah. I guess you're right about that. Like you said, 'one won't, another one will.'"

"That's my girl," Madame A says, patting my arm. "Let's get out of here. I know Cooter probably thinks I've run off with Fred since I'm taking so long to get to him."

"He does not, but do you think he would complain if he did?" I ask playfully.

"Nope. He ain't complaining 'cause he ain't looking to *hear* no complaints. Besides, they don't make rope thick enough to hold Cooter in one place long enough to complain."

"So it's just you and Mr. Smithey, now?"

"No, I didn't say that. Just 'cause you can't tie a man *down,* don't mean he don't want you to tie him *up* for a little while."

"But I thought…y'all got an understanding," I stammer in confusion.

"We do have an understanding. It's just that I don't want Cooter's viagra pills to expire before he can use them. They're pretty expensive I hear. Don't make no sense to let good medicine go to waste like that," she says with a straight face.

"Madame A, when I grow up, I want to be just like *you,*" I holler.

"Baby, put your running shoes on 'cause my tank is *always* on full."

Chapter

20 *Ten Years Later*

The sun beams hotly through the sunroof as we speed towards Madame A's house. It's her 85th birthday and they're throwing a huge party for her. Ten whole years since my "enlightening" Spring Break. And *what* years they have been.

When I got back to school after that Spring Break, the first thing I did have was what ended up being a *long* one-sided conversation with Stefan. After saying my piece, like a typical *boy*—definitely not a man—he said the stuff I was asking of him meant we were serious and he didn't know if we should be trying to get serious. Afterall, he wasn't looking to narrow his choice down to one woman right away. I thanked him for the unpleasant memories and walked away with my head held high. Within two weeks, I saw him walking around and holding hands, in the *daylight*, with his old girlfriend again. Goes to show you, what a man won't do for one, he'll *definitely* do for another. I guess she had higher standards than I did when I was dating him. Good riddance and I never looked back.

A whimpering in the rear seat breaks my thoughts and causes me to turn.

"What is it, baby?" I asked my cherubic one-year old son, Edgar. I turn in the seat, pat his head and ask, "You want some juice?"

"Baby, leave him alone. All that fussing over him gonna make him soft. He's fine. You know he don't like the car seat," my husband of two years, Ray Ray, says.

Yes, Ray Ray. Don't act surprised. It was written in the stars a long time ago. I had to run and waste plenty of time before all the lessons Madame A taught me sunk in and I realized it.

"Ray, he might be thirsty or something. I just don't know," I say, staring at my son, wishing that he was able to communicate effectively with me, not in baby language.

"We're gonna be there in a minute. Just hold on," Ray Ray says and pats my thighs, lovingly.

As we crest the hill, I see cars lined up along the drive and the sides of the road. It's definitely a full house with all these cars here. Ray Ray stops the car and we lift Edgar out of the car seat. My mother and father spot us and Edgar, his little legs churning, runs towards them.

"There's my baby!" my mother exclaims happily. Time has been very kind to her. Though there is a little more gray in her hair, the lines have not crowded and aged her face much.

"Hey, Del. Ray Ray," my father says, enveloping me in a big hug. "How was the trip?" Father Time missed my father also. Oh, more gray is sporting at the temples, but he still looks handsome as ever. Since he's retired from the plant, he's put on a few pounds from my mother's cooking.

"Good, Dad," Ray Ray says.

"Is Weenie here yet?" I ask excitedly. Weenie just finished architecture school and now lives in Atlanta.

"Not yet, but we're expecting him any minute." My mother says and resumes her 'baby talk' with Edgar.

"Who all is here?" I look back at the cars.

"Everybody and their moma, too!" my daddy says and laughs. "You'd think this was funeral repast with all these folks, not a birthday party."

"I'll bet Madame A is pretty excited," I say, walking towards the house.

"Yep. Fred's over there with her right now trying to fix plate of food for her."

"Mr. Fred's still in the picture after all these years." I say, shaking my head.

"Might as well not be, bad as she treats him. They never did get back on real good terms, but Fred don't seem to understand what 'No' means."

"At least she's still got some company. After Mr. Smithey died, I didn't think she would ever get back to her old self."

"That was a sad time for her, that's for sure. Though I didn't really agree with all her dating and stuff, I've got to say, it kept her going," my mother says, surprising me. All the opposition she put up when Madame A even *looked* like she was spending time with a man? Time *definitely* heals all wounds and shortens the memory.

We walk into the house and greet a multitude of people. I'm hugged and kissed and hugged some more by folks I know and some I didn't know. I finally spot Madame A out on the patio, a group of men around her. *Nothing's changed here, I see.* Mr. Fred sits within an arm's reach of her. I didn't know if he was sitting an arm's reach out because he was waiting to be helpful or just staying out of range of a backhand slap.

Madame A is a queen holding court. She has her hair up in a topknot, her makeup has been applied lightly and lipstick coats her mouth. She talks rapidly, her hands moving right along with her mouth. I didn't know what she told the group gathered around her, but they all broke out in laughter, that is, except for Mr. Fred. As someone doubles over, Madame A spots us and a huge grin divides her face. Rising, she grabs her cane and walks past her admirers and over to us.

"Del! Baby, come here!" she exclaims and I feel myself engulfed by short, flabby arms. "Baby, I'm so *glad* you could come!"

"Me too, Madame A, me too," I say, genuinely happy to see her.

"And look at you, Ray Ray. Boy, everytime I see you, you looking better and better." She fusses over him.

"That's 'cause Del takes such good care of me, like I do her." Ray hugs her and winks.

"That's the way it's supposed to be, too." She chuckles.

Seeing Edgar in Moma's arms, I watch as her eyes mist over and slowly she holds out her arms. Cooing as she holds him and hugs him, she has her eyes closed tightly, memories of another Edgar probably on her mind. Finally, she opens her eyes and looks at him. "Edgar. They sho' name you right 'cause you got a lot of your great-granddaddy in you."

Everyone is silent as she watches him. Surprisingly, Edgar just lays in her arms, staring into her eyes also. When he breaks into a toothy grin, everybody laughs at him.

"I told you that boy was gonna make some fine grandbabies, didn't I?" Madame A beams at me and says. "This baby's going somewhere. I can see it right now."

We leave him perched in her arms as we seek out food. Getting a plate, I return to Madame A and Edgar. He is playing with her cane and she is smiling at his antics. Mr. Fred smiles as he watches him play also.

"Madame A, you're sure looking gussied up today!" I say, admiringly.

"Baby, when you get my age, you've got to do a little more to get the same attention."

"And you're *still* getting attention, I see." I look at Mr. Fred.

"Gonna keep on until I die, I suspect. Hhmmp! I don't know why he keeps hanging around. I ain't thinking about his *old* ass," she says out of the side of her mouth.

I burst out laughing at that. "You think Ms. Bertha still is?" I whisper this question.

"Probably. I ain't heard that nobody else been spending time with her, so she probably still pining away, waiting for Fred to give her some attention," Madame A says, disgust in her voice.

"Is Mr. Cooter coming today?" Mr. Cooter did go back to St. Louis and from all accounts he has been pretty sick.

"Naw. You know he had a stroke and can't hardly get around much. He calls me from St. Louis and all but I don't think he has anybody to bring him out here."

"I hate that. I kinda wanted to see Mr. Cooter again."

"Well, that's the way life goes. You've got to use what you got as long as you can 'cause when it leaves you, it's gone for good."

"I'm glad it hadn't left you yet."

"Me too!" She chuckles again. "So, Del, ain't it amazing how life works out sometimes? You came to me that summer all worried about boys and was just about to miss your 'rough diamond' before I steered you in the right direction."

"I was not!"

"You were too. You had that young man up at school on the brain *bad*. If you hadn't of gotten some wisdom from me, your life could have been mighty different."

"Might have," I say, thinking about how Stefan really had some bad qualities when comparing him to Ray Ray.

"Yes, wasn't for your old grandmama, you'd be somewhere nursing a broken heart right about now."

"You're probably right about that, too."

"Yep. Seems like it's a woman's lot to spend time with folks that don't really mean her a bit of good and suffer along in the process."

"Well, I wish all of them had a Madame A to help them through. It sure would save plenty of time, energy and money if somebody would tell them how things really are supposed to be versus how the world expects us to act."

"Baby, one thing I learned about the world, it don't give a dog's butt about you and me. You've got to learn to take care of yourself *first* before you can take care of anything else."

"Tell me about it. Like you said, a woman's got to use her mojo."

"Del, when you've got your mojo working, can't nobody, and I mean *nobody,* resist you. And one thing I do know," she says, looking over at Mr. Fred who sits staring at her, "your grandmama's mojo *still* working."

"And you're a living testimony to that!"

THE END

Acknowledgements

Well guys, another book down! I think I'm really starting to feel my groove now. If you enjoyed this story, you might enjoy my others, available at my website: www.sydneymolare.com. I want to give thanks to God, my parents, siblings, extended family and friends who have supported my endeavors. Having strong family ties strengthens me and I am thankful. A great big smooch to my literary fans! I love ya!

Much gratitude to the ladies who entered the "Grandmama's Mojo Ain't *Nothing* Dead on Me!" contest. Congratulations to our winner and cover model, Mrs. Geneva Brown.

Now, before any of you critics and reviewers send me an email telling me Delphine is an "unbelievable character," I want you to take a look around your neighborhood and city/town/area. If you can't find a few girls who remind you of Delphine, sounds to me like you've got *much* work to do to change the *status quo*. Del is the role model!

To aspiring writers, don't give up the dream. If one company won't publish you, you can bet another one will. Everybody's got a story to tell and I, for one, would love to read yours. Take care and keep writing!

Sydney Molare'
www.sydneymolare.com
sydney@sydneymolare.com

COMING SOON!

Devil's Orchestra

Who's side are you *really* playing for?